Unwrapped

A *Camdyn Series* Christmas Novella

By

Christina Coryell

Books by Christina Coryell:

To Tammy,

Because I can't write a best friend story without thinking of you. Thank you for being mine.

Chapter One

"Officially the worst Christmas in the history of Christmases," I blurted, dropping my phone on the bed. Usually the drama in the room was provided by my best friend and roommate, but I couldn't seem to control my despair.

Camdyn half-closed the book she was reading, keeping her finger between the pages. "This I gotta hear."

"That was my mom. Apparently they're going to be spending Christmas in Florida with Aunt Shelly again."

"Bummer," Camdyn said, twisting her mouth sardonically to the side. "How will you ever get all the sand out of your bathing suit?"

I normally enjoyed her quick wit, but not so much when she employed it on me.

"You know I can't go to Florida. Don't you remember last year?"

Shudder—last year. Immediately upon our arrival at Aunt Shelly's condo, I was met by my new step-cousin Todd, who was all of fourteen and already six-foot-two. He quickly gave me a rundown on exactly how smokin' I was, and I spent the entire Christmas holiday avoiding that kid and sleeping with one eye open.

"Oh, yeah, the weirdo cousin. We all have one, don't we?" She paused, tilting her pretty blonde head to the side. "Except me, because I have no cousins. And that really has no bearing on your problem, so I digress."

Rising from my bed, I stepped over to the window of our dorm room and looked out onto the street, which was mostly deserted on that cold Missouri day. Letting out a sigh, I watched my breath fog the glass and then painted a little snowflake with my finger. Missouri doesn't always have white Christmases, but at least there was a chance. In Florida? Not so much.

I exhaled another heavy breath, which caught the attention of my roommate enough that she actually placed the book facedown on the bed. For the girl who always had her nose in her studies or a pen on the paper, that was quite a statement in and of itself.

Camdyn stepped up behind me and wrapped her arm around my shoulders. "I hate seeing you like this, and I don't want to hear any weird stories about Cousin Creepy when you come back to school. Why don't you come home with me?"

Go home with Camdyn? It would mean my first Christmas not spent with my parents. Not that home actually felt like home anymore, really.

Growing up, we made our home in Cape Girardeau, where my dad was a professor at Southeast Missouri State. Naturally, I chose to go to the University of Missouri, just so I wouldn't be picked out of the crowd because of my dad. He teasingly labeled me a traitor, but sometimes I wondered whether he was actually joking.

Last year, he took a position in Nebraska and my parents sold my childhood home. All of my Christmas memories were forevermore available solely in my mind due to the fact that random strangers now occupied my bedroom, my living room, and that totally perfect hollowed-out space across from the fireplace with the large bay windows. That was where a Christmas tree belonged, not in a rectangular Nebraska sitting room.

Having no Nebraska Christmas memories, my parents chose to spend that first holiday in the comfort of Aunt Shelly's new home, and I foolishly went along. Not only did Todd creep me out at every waking opportunity, but Aunt Shelly seemed insistent that we only eat seafood during that visit. Seafood is definitely not my first choice for Christmas. I like tradition, and our traditions included turkey, stuffing, and pumpkin pie.

Well, I was wise to the situation now, wasn't I? And I had a choice in the matter.

"Do you have pumpkin pie?" I asked as Camdyn slid her arm off my shoulders and leaned against the wall.

"Yeah, and my grandma's the absolute best cook. I promise you won't be disappointed."

"Okay," I agreed hesitantly, studying my friend. "What about Charlie, though? He won't mind?"

"Charlie?" Her amusement was short and to the point. "Don't be worried about Charlie. At worst, he might tease you like he does me. He'll probably ignore you, though. He'll be too good to socialize with us, since he's in school to become a pharmacist. I'm sure he'll be trying to lord it over me how wonderful he is."

She gave a quick eye roll, and I couldn't help but laugh. Being an only child, I didn't have an older brother to torment and tease me, so I wasn't sure how many of her stories were exaggerations.

"So, you in?"

Camdyn remained there with one foot on the floor and the other perched against the wall, looking every bit like one of those posters you see at the mall for clothing advertisements. Why God saw fit to pair me with a roommate who happened to be the most perplexing girl within a five mile radius was beyond me, but any hesitation I had upon first meeting her had long since melted away.

"How can I tell you no?" I reluctantly agreed, and she made a clicking noise with her tongue as she displayed a huge smile. "No, seriously, how? I'd really like to figure it out."

"You don't want to tell me no, because you know I'm right." Pulling herself away from the wall, she returned to her bed and picked up her book, setting it in her lap as she resumed her cross-legged position. "You'll miss your chance to see that guy, though...what was his name?"

"Philip?"

Admittedly, Philip was rather interesting. Not perfect or anything, mind you, but he kept me mildly distracted last year. We only saw him once, on Christmas Day when Aunt Shelly's brother-in-law from her previous marriage brought his kids over. Philip was a year younger than me, business major, liked to play rugby, and not entirely unattractive.

"Yeah, your Aunt Shelly's nephew, right?" Camdyn stated, the corners of her mouth drawing upward. "On second thought, you can't date your cousin's cousin. That's totally creepy."

"It's Christmas. I'm not looking to find the love of my life. I'd settle for good, old-fashioned caroling, trimming the tree, eating until I can't move..."

"Then you will definitely be in the right place, because there will be no one to date at all. It's a win-win for you."

"Very funny." I plopped down on my own bed. "What are you studying so intently over there?"

"Mao Tse-tung. This Chinese History class is going to be the death of me, since I've already had my grade docked. I absolutely have to be perfect on this final just to prove my point and to protest the blatant injustice that was perpetrated upon me."

Finding it impossible not to laugh, I attempted to hide it behind my fist. Camdyn was completely devoted to her studies and had to be the best academically, but the rest of the time she had a habit of being a rather overdramatic goofball.

"Would the world stop turning if Camdyn Taylor was rewarded a B in Chinese History?"

"It would be a blatant injustice," she repeated, not looking up from her book.

Poor Camdyn—she had been rather indignant over the Chinese History fiasco for a couple months, since her ex-boyfriend Blake showed up out of the blue in front of her class and proposed to her. The room erupted into laughter when she refused him and questioned his sanity, but the professor wasn't in a jovial mood. He vowed to dock her grade, and so far hadn't relented.

She'd been the target of misguided admiration after that incident with Blake Kennedy, because it took a unique woman to harness the attention of the handsome, aloof athlete. Not only did she manage to do just that, merely by tripping over the guy, but she also held him captive for months only to drop him like a hot rock at the end of the year. She thought they were just having a fling, but he didn't feel the same. Why the poor sap thought he should return to publicly humiliate himself by proposing was another story altogether.

"So do you think you're going to ace it, Miss Smarty Pants?" It was nearly impossible for me not to goad her, since she was constantly on my back about studying.

We were polar opposites, Camdyn and me. I rarely ever bothered to crack the books outside of class. My life was usually quite normal and routine, while Camdyn was a disaster waiting to happen. We even looked like opposites, with her naturally wavy blonde hair versus my own milk-chocolate-brown, straight-as-a-board variety. We completed each other's weaknesses in the best ways, though.

"Of course," she stated breezily. "I have a whole scenario in my head where I've imagined that I'm an impoverished Chinese woman. My husband has recently died and I'm alone with my baby, so things are rather difficult."

"You and your imagination. You should write books about those stories in your head."

7

"I prefer to keep them in my head where I can tweak them and improve them." Leaning forward, her face grew serious. "I have a close friend who has inside dealings with the Kuomintang. We've been forbidden to have a relationship, but our affections for one another cannot be quelled. I fear there will be a revolution soon, and my love will be unrequited. Dear God, don't let my love perish!"

Biting my lip, I tried not to laugh at her wide blue eyes. "Perish in the revolution?"

"No." Going back to her previous posture, she brought her book up toward her face. "Perish in the clutches of a disastrously undeserved grade."

Chapter Two

"*B* Plus!" Throwing her duffel bag into the trunk of my red two-door coupe, Camdyn turned to me again with her hands on her hips. "Can you believe it? The nerve of that man! I guarantee you he proposed to some woman early in his life and she turned him down, so he's taking it out on me."

She had been going on about her grade for a solid hour. If some professor had given me a B on my final, I would have been hugging him after class and jumping up and down. Some crazy antagonistic professor decided to give Camdyn a B, and suddenly the only option was to drive *my* car to her grandmother's. If I would have allowed her to drive in her mental state, it might have diminished our chances of making it to St. Louis alive.

"He's decided I'm the poster child for misplaced devotion." Pulling the passenger door closed behind her, Camdyn linked her fingers behind her head and stared at the sunroof. "I should launch a complaint against him on behalf of all women who have been saddled with undesirable proposals. As though I wanted Blake to interrupt the class and tell me that I was his soul's running partner. Yick. If he wanted to propose, he should have at least done it eloquently and properly. And he might have done a little research into whether the girl was interested or not."

"Well, maybe you'll get lucky and no one will ever propose to you again."

"I should hope not."

She stretched the seat belt across her abdomen and planted the soles of her tennis shoes against the dash with her knees against her chest, her pink sweats reaching just to the top of her shins. Not telling her to remove her feet from the dash took every ounce of patience in my body.

Ignoring my motherly instincts about the car made me shake my head a little as I pondered our different quests in life. My idyllic plans consisted of settling down in the suburbs, raising a couple kids, going to recitals, cheering at ball practices, and cooking gourmet meals for my wealthy doctor husband. (That last part was just a suggestion.)

The fact that dreams weren't guaranteed to become realities didn't stop me from comparing my situation to Camdyn's. I wouldn't have minded having someone propose to me in history class. (Not that I would take Chinese history...too many facts to remember.) If I had even one iota of affection for the guy, I would have probably said yes. Unlike my cynical companion, I was a sucker for romance.

"Oh, by the way, Charlie's not very happy with me for inviting you to Christmas."

Naturally she waited until I started the car to inject *that* tidbit of information. Twisting my head in her direction, I allowed my mouth to drop open.

"Are you kidding me? What am I supposed to do with that?"

"Relax," she said, dragging her feet down from the dash. "I explained the weird cousin situation, and the whole aversion to seafood, and he understands."

"You told Charlie about Todd?" Even in the chill of the below-freezing day, my fingers threatening to fuse like ice to the steering wheel as my car attempted to bring the heat up to a useful temperature, I could feel the burning in my cheeks.

"Um, yeah, to do you a favor. Don't worry, it mellowed him out. Besides, he was only annoyed because he said it was his time to relax and unwind, and he thought he might have to entertain you."

Whenever Camdyn brought up her brother, I tried to walk a fine line of moderate interest without getting too involved. One of the worst stories she ever told me was about her thirteenth birthday, when she invited some girls over for a sleepover. She found out when she went back to school on Monday that they only agreed to come because they wanted to see Charlie. She had a hard time trusting friends after that point, and I could hardly blame her. Camdyn and I had been thick as thieves from day one, and I was her friend because she was the milk to my Oreos. The peanut butter to my jelly. That unique person I could go without seeing for a month and know we would pick up right where we left off, finishing each other's sentences.

Still, the thought of Charlie believing I was an idiotic, flaky friend of his kid sister set me on edge. Even though we hadn't met, I'd spoken to him on the phone. He had an easy, pleasant timbre to his voice, and seemed genuinely nice. Camdyn had given me all sorts of information about him, and despite the fact that she told me about the many goofy things they had done over the years, I knew that he had to be at least semi-serious, since he was studying to be a pharmacist.

"As though you'd want to be entertained by Charlie," Camdyn added as she stared out the window, giggling to herself.

♥

"I'm home!" Camdyn called as she threw open the front door, dropping her bag to the floor. The scent of cinnamon swam toward me through the air, overwhelming my senses as I pulled the door closed behind me. My friend was off like a light, nearly sprinting into the adjoining kitchen, leaving me standing in the entryway awkwardly clinging to my blue paisley suitcase like I was waiting for the concierge to return to the hotel lobby. Deciding I might as well try to follow her, rather than stand there all day, I placed my suitcase on the carpet and stepped further into the delicious smell.

"Oh, I missed you so much," I heard from a voice that was soft, light, and full of emotion. This house was old-fashioned, marked by olive-green appliances, worn linoleum, delicious aromas of food cooking, and quiet, loving voices to welcome her home. It was very Mayberry-esque.

My mind drifted to the homes I had known. The one in Cape Girardeau was filled with rich, dark woods, my father's musty old books, and the scent of lemon furniture polish. The only thing uncertain in that house was whether I might slide across the floor when I stepped off the stairs onto the hardwood with my socked feet.

That scene faded, and the house in Nebraska began to push its way into my mind. Pristine and lifeless, those same books not yet unpacked from their boxes, with white carpet, stainless steel appliances, and a slight whistle from the vents when the heat or air conditioning kicked on. Like a sanitary hospital scene, really—a veritable insane asylum. If I sat there in the silence long enough, listening to the hum of the ductwork, it was quite possible I would go out of my mind.

No wonder Mom and Dad wanted to go to Florida for Christmas.

"This must be the beautiful Trina I've heard so much about."

Rapid blinking in response was probably not the most polite way to greet Camdyn's grandmother, but hearing my name had startled me out of my mental reverie.

"I'm so glad to finally meet you, Mrs. Taylor," I said as she stepped toward me, a warm smile lighting her face. I had expected Camdyn's grandmother to be petite, blonde, and rather boisterous. Instead, she was rail thin and taller than my friend, very soft spoken with a mass of dark silver curls bouncing to her shoulders.

"Please, call me Willa," she insisted as she moved past my outstretched hand and pulled me into a warm hug, squeezing me gently. "Thank you so much for being a good friend to my girl."

Whether it was from the whole Mayberry vibe I had noticed a moment before, or the fact that I was feeling a bit sentimental about missing my old home, or simply because Camdyn's grandmother smelled like a mix of roses and vanilla, I nearly lost it. In fact, my eyes were stinging so fiercely, I'm still a little amazed that I didn't start sobbing right on the poor woman's shoulder.

"I love her," I mumbled.

Yes, I told Willa Taylor that I loved her granddaughter, like a complete buffoon. To make matters worse, while I was mentally cringing and wishing I could turn back the hands of time, she merely patted me on the back like one would comfort a child.

"I know you do, honey."

Oh, the agony.

"Aw, Trina, I love you back," Camdyn added while she plucked a couple red grapes from a bowl on the counter, grinning at me like I had just fallen out of a loaded clown car.

"Something smells great," I said, hoping to change the subject.

"It's Grandma's cinnamon bread," Camdyn was quick to inform me, standing near the oven as she made a show of inhaling. "It's so good to be home. We eat like peasants."

"Not really," I added.

Willa offered a wink to ensure me that she knew we were properly fed. "I'm sure you girls are glad to have your semester over. How are your studies?"

My insides clenched as I prepared myself for another onslaught of despair over a B plus. Rather than go off on a tirade, however, Camdyn simply shrugged her shoulders and said things were pretty good. Apparently Willa had a calming presence, which was plenty intriguing and curiously soothing. Maybe this *was* precisely where I should spend my holidays.

"It's December 20th," Camdyn announced, wrapping her arm around her grandmother's waist and leaning her head against her arm. "Did you start without me?"

"Would I do that?" Willa patted Camdyn's hand and nodded her head in the direction of the refrigerator. "Pull out the eggs, sweetie."

"Growing up we had an advent calendar for *every* day of December," Camdyn explained as she opened the refrigerator. "Instead of finding chocolate or an ornament behind the doors, each day had a different Christmas tradition. The 20th is sugar cookies, and we take them to all our neighbors when we're finished." Turning to place the eggs on the counter, Camdyn pressed her backside against the cabinets and smiled. "Did you do yesterday's, Grandma?"

"Of course I did, but it wasn't the same without you."

Shoving my hands in my jeans pockets in an attempt to push back my sudden feelings of being an outsider, I stood awkwardly in the kitchen. Always perceptive, Camdyn was quick to catch my eye.

"On the 19th we make our own wreath. I'm sorry we missed it. We go to this farm out of town that Grandma used to live near when she was a girl. She still keeps in touch with the owners, even though it's passed hands three times. We use cedar and ribbon and never make it the same way twice. But I didn't see it on the door when we came in." Camdyn directed the last bit at her grandmother, who simply smiled before answering.

"No, it's still in the living room on the table. I thought you might want to hang it."

Glancing into the living room from the edge of the kitchen, Camdyn wrinkled her nose.

"You sure you made that yourself? That looks way better than it does when I help you."

I nearly laughed out loud when Willa looked at me again. That statement didn't surprise me in the least, because Camdyn didn't have a crafty bone in her body. Not really any coordinated bones, come to think of it. How she managed to run every morning without killing herself was beyond me.

We stood there comfortably in the kitchen, the three of us mixing cookie dough and chatting, with Willa making every effort to ensure I was involved in their tradition. It made me think about my own family.

Had I been home (actually home in Cape Girardeau, not in the pristine new sanitarium in Nebraska), Mom would have been lining up social functions for her neighborhood groups and Dad would have been buried in whatever paper he was writing. We didn't really have a crafty, homemade, make-your-own-cookies type of holiday. Things were catered and delivered and planned in advance.

Cooking held a definite allure for me, though. I'd always loved making a mess in the kitchen trying to create new culinary delights. Over the years I had managed to pull off a few great dishes, so I knew with practice I could be a sufficient cook.

"Now, things have to chill," Willa stated as she took the large yellow mixing bowl and placed plastic wrap over the top, shifting it to the refrigerator. She pulled out three red bowls that she had waiting inside, placing them on the counter.

Cutting out the endless rolls of sugar cookies took most of the afternoon, and as we neared the end of the dough in the red bowls, I reached for the refrigerator door to retrieve the yellow bowl. Catching my eye, Willa shook her head. I hardly blamed her, because I was growing tired of cutting out the cookies myself, and she already had several plates of them on the counter.

"I'm going to go wash all this flour off," Camdyn announced as she finished. "Trina, you want me to show you around?"

"I'll find it in a second," I assured her as she passed me on her way to the hall. While I tidied up my little corner and wiped up the remains of flour, I glanced at Willa, who was poking into the refrigerator again. Without a word, she grabbed the yellow bowl and promptly dumped the contents into the trash, covering the mess with some crumpled paper towels. Intrigued, I forgot to pretend that I wasn't watching, and I stood there gawking at her strange actions.

"Oh." She startled as she turned and saw me staring. "Don't tell her."

I almost giggled, but thought better of the action. Twisting my mouth to the side, I stepped a smidge closer. "What are you doing?"

"Have you ever had any food Camdyn prepared?" she whispered. Taking a second to consider her question, I slowly shook my head. "Well, neither will the neighbors if I can help it."

Chapter Three

By the time the evening began to wind down, an unexpected calm had come over me. It was unclear whether I should attribute my laid-back attitude to Willa's attentive pampering, which I was enjoying to the fullest, or to the fact that Camdyn herself seemed rather mellow in this environment, which almost never happened in our normal day to day lives.

Just to make sure an alien hadn't abducted my friend when we arrived at the doorstep, I glanced over to where she sat on the couch a few feet from me, eyeing her with curiosity.

"So, are you going to protest your Chinese history grade?"

Letting out a sigh, she pressed her wrist against her temple and closed her eyes for a second. "Probably won't do any good. I'll worry about it later."

Uh huh. Alien abduction.

"Girls, I think I'm going to turn in. Do you have everything you need?" Willa waited at the edge of the room, appearing tired. I couldn't help but wonder whether whatever brought about Camdyn's mellow mood was causing the opposite effect on her grandmother, and all the extra attention was making her weary. Mentally I vowed to help her a bit more the next day.

"Don't worry, Grandma. I'll take perfect care of Trina."

Camdyn shot me a wink before she bounced up off the couch and stepped toward her grandmother, wrapping her arms around the older woman like she never wanted to let go. When she finally released her, she kissed her grandmother's cheek.

"Good night, Grandma. Love you."

"Love you too, sweetie. Good night, Trina."

"Good night," I called, watching Camdyn as she returned to plop down beside me.

Letting out all of her breath in a rush, she closed her eyes and rested her head against the couch. "I'm glad you're here. So much better than spending time on the beach, am I right?"

"Naturally." Shaking my head, I allowed a small smile to escape. "Your grandma's wonderful."

Camdyn peeked out of one eye at me while she pursed her lips in mock frustration. "How many times have I told you that, Trina? Are you saying you don't trust me?"

Laughing, I rose and stretched my arms behind my head, releasing a deep yawn. "I'm saying a good night's sleep sounds pretty great right now."

"Deflecting the question. That's okay, I won't press the subject. You want to sleep in Charlie's room?"

"No," I blurted, eyes widening. "You said Charlie didn't even want me here, so why would I want to take over his bedroom?"

"He won't be here for two days. Anyway, it's not like he's been sleeping in there, so you don't have to worry about it being gross."

Leave it to Camdyn to think I'm worried about her brother being gross.

"Are you sure he won't mind?"

"What he doesn't know won't hurt him, right?"

She prefaced that question with a mischievous smile, which made me feel slightly rebellious. Camdyn stood and jerked her head toward the hallway, which I took as a nonverbal instruction to follow her. Just a few feet into the hall, she turned into the open doorway that framed her bedroom, pausing by the suitcase I had placed there earlier. Glancing at the rows of books on the shelves along the wall and the colorful portraits of landscapes and city scenes gracing nearly every inch of the room, I took a second to study my friend.

"What?" she asked.

"Riddle me this, Batman. How do you come across so..." Pausing, I measured my words carefully, "...normal?"

"Normal?" There was no mistaking the stink-eye she was giving me at that moment.

"You have all the appearances of being cool and trendy, but you're sort of a nerd."

"How dare you call me 'sort of' a nerd?" Grabbing a pair of fake reading glasses off her nightstand, she perched them atop her nose and struck a little pose. The fact that Camdyn's attempt at being goofy made her look like a model in a Gap ad was not lost on me. So obnoxiously unfair. "For the record, I'm a total nerd. I thought you would have known that by now."

"Why do you have fake glasses?"

"They make me look smart."

Of course.

"What's with all the pictures on the wall?"

"Places I want to go," she told me, removing the glasses from her face and placing them back on the nightstand. "Athens, Egypt, Moscow, Amazon rainforest, Smoky Mountains, Wrigley Field..."

"One of these things is not like the others."

"Oh, I have no fascination with Wrigley Field. I just want to wear Cardinals red there to taunt the Cubbies."

Glancing at her rows of books, I raised my eyebrows. "So you fill your room with places you want to go, and..."

"...places I've already been." She grinned at her books, as though they held some secret treasure map. It was the same look she got on her face in our dorm room when she was scribbling notes about her history courses. The girl had a more active imagination than me, if she viewed books as taking her to faraway lands. I preferred to actually see things in front of me, rather than reading about them in books.

Grabbing my suitcase, I carried it into the hall, waiting as she followed me and then turned to the bedroom across the way. Pushing the door wide, she waited as I stepped inside and gasped. The entire space was full of baseball memorabilia, with signed balls on the dresser, a couple replica statues, two or three rather worn-out gloves, and a white bedspread with red stitching in a circular pattern.

"Does Charlie play baseball?" I stared at the splashes of red that dotted the room in the form of St. Louis Cardinals logos.

"No, he just really likes it. Don't worry about it, but don't touch anything. He would notice, trust me. He's really protective about his stuff."

Great.

"So, you good?" she continued. "Cause I could turn in."

"Go ahead."

Camdyn was notorious for going to bed before me, mostly because she got up at the crack of dawn for her morning runs. Occasionally I talked her into staying up with me, watching Leno and eating Oreos, but most of the time I was solo.

Not wanting to make much noise in the house with both Willa and Camdyn going to bed, I settled my suitcase on the foot of my sleeping area, retrieved my pajamas and prepared for the earlier-than-normal bedtime.

♥

A mist rose over the Ozark Mountains, thick and foreboding as it pulled me farther into the darkness, the damp air clinging to my clothes. As I struggled to push away, the nearby foothills turned into piles of books, stacked haphazardly as far as the eye could see. The thought began to circulate in my mind that I needed to find a way back, but I couldn't force my lips to form the words.

As I looked around for an escape, something crashed against my body, leaving me feeling scared and confused. My breath began coming in short bursts, and I felt the onset of panic. Before my brain could begin to react, I heard a low groan beside me, and my eyes flew open, trying to adjust to the darkness and remember where I was.

Camdyn's grandma's house...her brother's bedroom. As the realization of my location flooded me, I realized the fact that the bed moved slightly, and something large and bulky just connected with my leg. Reaching out hesitantly, my fingers connected with something that definitely shouldn't have been there.

Fear gripping my chest, I shoved against the bulk, feeling it move away from my middle and further toward my knees. The fact that I managed to move it did little to calm me, though, because I had determined in those moments that it was real and not part of my Ozark Mountains dream. Thrashing my legs, I swung my arm wide, hoping to clear myself of whatever was in the bed.

"What the..."

Even as the male voice met my ears, the bed shifted again underneath me, and I heard the thud of something hitting the floor right before the light came on overhead, flooding the room and temporarily blinding me.

Blinking to try to clear the fuzz from my sight, I managed to focus on the startling figure by the door.

"Funny. Grandma's never given me a gift like this before. What did she promise you, a green card?"

The athletic-looking guy in front of me grinned, showcasing a nice smile that lit up his face and brought a shine to his blue eyes. Pausing to run his fingers through his blond hair, he laughed.

"I know she wants me to find a nice girl, but I didn't think she'd actually resort to finding me a mail order bride. Where did you come from? Latin America? Eurasia?" He tilted his head as he stared at me, folding his arms across his chest. "It's not every day that a guy comes home to find a beautiful woman in his bed. I'm a little stunned."

My eyes drifted to the foot of the bed, where a large black bag rested, and my foggy mind attempted to put the facts together. The bag was most likely thrown on the bed, where he sat beside me. Since he still had his shoes on, and his jeans, and a St. Louis Cardinals T-shirt, he couldn't have been there long. As I realized with clarity what was happening, I struggled to release myself from the baseball bed sheets, trying to stand.

"Relax, Trina," he stated. "I'm just messing with you. I should have called to tell them I'd be home earlier than I expected. Sorry for the rude wake-up call, but keep the bed. I don't mind sleeping on the couch." As though he intended to punctuate his words, he stepped back toward the bed, picked up the overflowing duffel bag and slung it over his shoulder. "And don't worry, I won't let any intruders in the house." At that, he had the audacity to wink at me before he opened the door and stepped back into the hallway as he flipped the light switch, closing me in the darkness once again.

My heart immediately started overreacting, because what started out as a weird dream inspired by Camdyn's bedroom had turned into a few startling revelations:

Number one—Charlie Taylor was incredibly handsome.

Number two—he might have been partially teasing, but he *did* call me beautiful.

And number three—the insane pounding in my chest at that moment had almost nothing to do with the fear of intruders.

Chapter Four

Willa offered to make pancakes in the morning, but I insisted she shouldn't go to the trouble. Camdyn didn't want a heavy breakfast since she just finished her morning run. Charlie was in the shower so he couldn't vote, and I hated to ask her to make breakfast for me. When she finally admitted that she had cereal, I assured her that was perfectly fine. She directed me to one of the higher cabinets, where I pulled open the door to find a couple sensible varieties of whole bran, along with a few full-sugar options that I hadn't thought about since I'd been six or seven years old.

Stifling a giggle, I felt a presence beside me, and I glanced over to see Charlie, hair still damp from the shower, wearing a navy-blue tee with the requisite Cardinal in the center. Without a word or a peek in my direction, he reached past my shoulder and wrapped his fingers around a brightly colored box.

"Charlie, can't you even introduce yourself and be polite?" Camdyn scolded from her seat at the kitchen table, where she twisted a half-full glass of orange juice in her hands. "Honestly, Trina, you're so lucky you're an only child."

Placing the box of cereal on the counter, Charlie let out a loud sigh before he turned to face me. "Charles David Taylor. It's an honor to make your acquaintance. May I interest you in some Fruity Pebbles?"

"You're really eating those?" I asked, glancing at the box.

"Sort of." Removing another box from the cabinet, he placed it in front of me. "The mix is the thing...half Fruity Pebbles, half Lucky Charms. Delicious."

My gut instinct told me that he was teasing me again, but when he retrieved a bowl and began pouring both cereals together, I could see he was serious. While he opened the refrigerator and removed the milk, he met my eye and offered a rather crooked smile.

"I'm not really sure you know how the whole introduction scenario works. I told you my name...my full, proper name...so I think you're supposed to reciprocate."

My lips ached to offer a smile, but in front of Camdyn's prying eyes, I didn't dare. "Trina Justine Miller, and I'm familiar with how to make a proper introduction, thank you."

"Might I interest you in cereal heaven, Miss Miller?" He held the milk carton toward me with that mischievous look on his face, and a warm feeling spread across my neck, leaving me feeling more than a little embarrassed.

"Don't listen to him, Trina. That's so gross."

Pulling out an extra bowl, he gave me one more look, his blue eyes sparkling in the early morning light filtering through the window. "Come on," he whispered. "You know you want to try it."

He was totally wrong about that—I absolutely didn't want to try it. Still, for whatever insane reason, I found myself absently nodding my head like an imbecile, and then watching in clear disgust as he dumped that concoction into a bowl. Once the milk was poured over the top of the colorful marshmallows and the bright puffs of cereal, he handed the bowl to me, lowering himself to a chair at the kitchen table.

"What happened to your face?" Camdyn inspected him carefully, narrowing her eyes at her brother.

Shoving a spoonful of cereal into his mouth, he hesitated as he stared up at the ceiling, most likely preparing an excuse. I took the opportunity to stare at his profile, noticing the light bruise on his cheekbone that Camdyn was referencing.

"Funny story, actually," he finally stated. "I got into a bit of a scuffle last night."

"*You* got into a fight." Judging by the look on Camdyn's face, she didn't believe his story.

Charlie twisted his face so he was looking at me, and he offered a hint of a smile. "Yeah, it wasn't a big deal. Misunderstanding mostly, and I couldn't get out of the way fast enough."

"Some guy hit you," Camdyn attempted to clarify.

"Yep." He nodded, scooping up another spoonful of cereal. "Big guy. Really big, burly guy."

I didn't offer any comment, since I was fairly certain I was the one who had given Charlie the mark on his otherwise flawless face. I covered my awkwardness by shoveling a spoon's worth of that cereal into my mouth. The mix of a million different forms of sugar competed for attention on my taste buds, and I cringed.

"You don't have to eat that, honey." Willa moved up behind me and rested her hand on my shoulder. Charlie shot me a challenging look, and I sat up a little straighter.

"Thanks, but it's fine." Normally I wasn't one for lying, but something inside was telling me to stand up to him. Doing so for the sake of a bowl of cereal seemed pretty idiotic, but I didn't want him to get the best of me.

"What are you girls doing today?" Charlie wanted to know, crunching on that cereal concoction like it was delicious. I forced another bite down my throat, pretending I wasn't about to go into sugar shock.

"Girl stuff," Camdyn answered, shaking her head. "Aren't you going to hang out with your friends?"

"I want to hang out with you. I cleared my calendar so I could entertain your friend, just like you asked."

"Aw, that would be sweet of you, if 'leave us alone' sounded anything like 'entertain Trina,' which it doesn't. Nice try."

"I apologize to you," Charlie added, looking at me with a rather sad expression. "You probably came here expecting to have fun, but Camdyn is determined to keep you away from your only possible source of excitement."

"Don't let him sweet talk you, Trina. He's just being ridiculous." She turned her eyes to her brother in exasperation. "Leave her alone, would you?"

"What's the 21st?" I asked, attempting to break the tension.

"The 21st what?" Camdyn questioned.

"You know, the 19th was the wreath, the 20th was the cookies, so the 21st is..."

"Charlie's birthday," Willa answered from behind me, pulling out a chair and settling at the table with her own bowl of whole wheat, nutritious cereal. In my innermost thoughts, I was tempted to steal it to avoid the impending cavities.

"It's your birthday?" My eyebrows drew together as I focused my attention on Charlie. "I had no idea. Happy birthday."

"Thanks," he told me with a smile, dropping the spoon into his empty bowl. "Technically it was my birthday last night too, when I was attacked. Not really a nice way to treat a guy on his birthday."

"Take that up with the guy who hit you," Camdyn muttered, placing her elbows on the table.

"If it's Charlie's birthday, shouldn't you do what he wants?" My suggestion didn't go over well with Camdyn, who widened her eyes.

"I like you already," Charlie stated with a grin as he rose from his chair and began to pour more cereal into his bowl. How he planned on cramming down more of that sugary breakfast was beyond me.

"Don't feel sorry for him, Trina," Camdyn said. "After Charlie time, he always disappears, and I'm sure today will be no different."

"What's Charlie time?" I asked as he took his seat beside me at the table.

"We watch 'A Charlie Brown Christmas' every year," Willa answered. "It used to come on television, but the last few years we've made a point of watching it on Charlie's birthday."

"They hold me here against my will." Charlie's words captured my attention, which instantly seemed like a mistake as those blue eyes threatened to hold me hostage.

"You don't feel bad about skipping out on your poor grandmother?" I teased, trying to ignore the seriousness in his gaze.

"I don't skip out. Camdyn's exaggerating because she wants to change the subject so you don't find out about the crying."

"The crying?"

"Sure, she cries like a baby when she watches Charlie Brown. He reminds her of herself, you know."

"Knock it off." Camdyn reached across the small table to poke him in the shoulder. "Trina knows me way better than you think, so she won't believe your lies."

He began eating his cereal again, and I pushed around the contents of my own colorful bowl, which had quickly become a soggy mess.

"You know, Cam, you really are a great sister. I think I should go Christmas shopping today and buy you a fantastic gift."

Those words were unexpected enough that all of our eyes shot to Charlie at once.

"That's nice, Charlie," Willa stated with obvious pride.

"What do you say, Trina, are you up for it?" There was no mischievousness in Charlie's eyes as they stared into mine, awaiting my response.

"How do you expect me to go shopping with you if you're buying a gift for me?" Camdyn said.

"I didn't ask you, I asked Trina."

"She doesn't want to do that," she quickly answered. Too quickly, because I was still wrapping my mind around his question.

"Actually, I could probably do a little shopping myself," I lied. Camdyn's present was in my suitcase, and I'd had it since October. Procrastination was not one of my personality traits.

"See? Look at me, doing your friend a favor. You really should thank me, sis."

"You're a piece of work," she told him, dragging her gaze from Charlie to me with clear disappointment. "Whatever. If you really think you need to go shopping, I guess I'd rather you were with Charlie than traipsing about by yourself."

I probably should have been mildly insulted by that comment, but *I'd rather you were with Charlie* was translating in my mind to *please hang out with my gorgeous brother*. Why hadn't my best friend ever bothered to tell me that her brother was incredibly good looking?

"I'm going to try really hard to be nice to you since it's your birthday," Camdyn continued, "but don't pull any funny business with Trina. I mean it."

"What do you think I'm going to do, leave her at the mall?" He turned to me then and winked, and I averted my eyes for fear that Camdyn might be able to read my thoughts.

"You know very well what I mean, Charlie. No funny business."

Chapter Five

*C*harlie Taylor was at least five-foot-eleven and was built like one of those soccer players my dad used to watch on television. Not that I was trying to notice, but I couldn't help but admire him as he helped Willa move the couch over a couple feet, or peek at him while he was watching the morning newscast, or study him every time his lips moved. Truth be told, I was flat-out staring at him like an infatuated preteen, trying to hide it and praying that Camdyn wouldn't discover my fascination. To my knowledge, she hadn't.

When it neared lunch time, Charlie announced he was ready to head out, and I grabbed my purse and my coat, hurriedly stepping into the bathroom to check my appearance one last time. Making an attempt to look my absolute best would have been my play had I been back at school preparing for a date, but Camdyn would have noticed my efforts and discovered my intentions. In fact, a week before she would have called me out for having a crush on Charlie, but here in her grandmother's house, she wasn't as observant as usual.

"Bring her back in one piece, Chuck," Camdyn called as we headed out the front door.

"Good grief," he countered, shaking his head. "She knows I hate that. You're lucky to be an only child."

I stepped up to the passenger side of his black sedan, pulling the door open and sliding inside. The warm scents of coffee and vanilla wafted toward me, and I glanced at the console, noting two insulated cups in the cup holders.

"Sorry about the mess," he said as he closed himself inside the small space next to me. "I drank a lot of coffee last night to keep myself awake."

My eyes drifted to the backseat, where I saw a few more to-go cups with the telltale lids scattered on the floorboard.

"That's an insane amount of coffee."

"That's not all from last night. I drink a lot of coffee when I'm studying."

"In the car?"

Sighing, he placed his hands on the steering wheel and offered a lopsided grin. "I drink a lot of coffee, period. Satisfied, Sherlock?"

"Whatever you say, Chuck. How did you know I was an only child?"

Turning the key in the ignition, he glanced up to his rear view mirror before backing out of the driveway. "I know many things about you. You're Camdyn's favorite topic of conversation, outside of history, grades, and whatever guy is annoying her at the moment."

Peeling my eyes away from him, I stared out the passenger window. The fact that he knew things about me was slightly terrifying. Camdyn had talked about Charlie's goofy attributes, and told me stories about them as kids, but she never mentioned that he was witty or charming or handsome. Suddenly I wondered if she had done the same while talking about me. *Oh, Trina's such a big goofball. Always insists on eating Oreos in bed. Never takes her studies seriously. Thinks she has to constantly be on the lookout for a boyfriend.*

I could practically feel my blood going cold in my veins at the thought.

"So, your parents are going to Florida for Christmas, right?"

"Yes, to visit my aunt."

"And what about Ash?"

"Ash?" Wrinkling my nose, I turned toward him. "What is that supposed to mean?"

"Sorry, I just thought I'd be polite and ask. If you don't want to talk about it, no problem. Seat belt."

He grasped the front of his seat belt and pulled it back slightly, snapping it into place. Taking his suggestion, I reached for my own safety device, tugging it across my chest.

"I have no opinion one way or the other, because I honestly don't understand your Ash reference."

"Your boyfriend, the football player? Everyone just calls him by his last name?"

It would have been easy to tell Charlie that I had no boyfriend, knew no one named Ash, and hadn't been out with a football player since high school. For whatever reason, I chose to hold that information in my back pocket for a minute.

"You know everything about my love life?" I shot him an accusatory glare, and for a split second he looked like he might want to backpedal. Instead, he shrugged his shoulders.

"Just what Cam told me."

"When did she tell you about Ash?"

"Last summer."

"Last summer?" I almost gasped out a laugh, but composed myself just in time. Right before summer break, Camdyn broke up with Blake and I officially swore off dating, a sort of pact between us not to settle for less than Mr. Right. I made it a whole three weeks before I went to the movies with Porter McClain, but I never admitted that to Camdyn. "Why was she even telling you about that?"

"She had a picture of the two of you on her dresser."

"Me and Ash?"

"No, you and Camdyn. I happened to see it and asked if it was you, and she promptly told me that you had a boyfriend. Football player, goes by his last name, really intimidating guy..."

The laughter couldn't be held back any longer, and I brought my hand up to my mouth to try to conceal it.

"All that just because you asked if the picture was of me?"

"Mostly." The bottom of his cheek started to flush, and I knew instinctively he wasn't being honest. Camdyn always blushed when she got uncomfortable too, naturally aided by her light coloring.

"Tell me the truth."

His eyes darted to me for a split second before he returned his attention to the road, a muscle working in his jaw.

"I might have said something," he admitted, draping his arm nonchalantly over the steering wheel. "Maybe something like...huh. Oh. Wow..."

"Huh." I turned my face to the passenger window again so I could hide my smile.

"So, what does Trina Justine Miller want out of life? To become a professional cheerleader for the Dallas Cowboys? Cure cancer? Be hired as an executive of some company?"

"I'm working toward a degree in Elementary Education."

He turned the car away from the sleepy road onto a busy intersection.

"That's what you're doing, not what you want—two different questions. Is that your dream, to be a teacher?"

"Part of it, I guess."

"Then lay it on me, no holding back."

Biting the corner of my lip, I prepared to say the brutally honest words that would terrify nearly every male my own age.

"I'd like to work with kids, meet a nice guy, get married, find a house in the suburbs, and be a really great mom."

And...that should send him running for the hills. Good thing I've got Ash to fall back on.

"Huh."

"Huh." I cringed just a bit.

"That's a pretty specific list, but admirable. Speaking as a guy who didn't have a mom, I like your goals."

"Don't patronize me."

"I'm not," he said, holding one hand in the air as though surrendering. "You mentioned meeting a nice guy, so I assume that means you haven't locked in on the candidate?"

He took the opportunity to smile in my direction, and I let my guard down.

"I've always imagined myself marrying a doctor," I teased.

He raised his eyebrows as he drew the car to the right, heading off the interstate.

"You know, I'm in the process of earning my Doctor of Pharmacy degree right now. It's my last year at UNC. Not that it matters about the whole doctor thing. Just thought I'd throw that out there."

As he was checking for oncoming traffic, I used the opportunity to study his profile. Charlie would certainly make an attractive doctor. I could imagine some of the girls back at school faking an illness so they could go to the emergency room if he was on call. To be honest, I could imagine myself doing that.

But would I get a flu shot simply to see the pharmacist?

Peeling my eyes away from his face, I realized it would be awfully tempting.

"What made you go to North Carolina?" I asked, driving the conversation away from my guilty conscience.

"One of the best pharmacy schools in the country. And I wanted to get out of the Lou for a while to stretch my horizons. Once I'm back, I'll be here for good."

"Devoted to 'the Lou' for the rest of your life?"

He smiled at my use of the nickname for his city. "I don't know. I have to stick around for Grandma, and once Camdyn's out of college I'll most likely stay to keep an eye on her. When your family consists of three people, you have to stick together."

"You think she'll come back to St. Louis? I'm pretty sure she wants to travel the world."

"Heaven help the world then." He laughed as he gave me a charming grin, but then cleared his throat. "Don't get me wrong. I love my sister, and I'd do absolutely anything for her, but she gets herself into some messes. Usually I'm the one who has to pull her out of them, although I'd guess you've probably performed your share of rescues."

"She can be dramatic, sure, but I don't know how I would have survived without her. My roommate before her was really messy, and she never takes my toothpaste."

"Because she has fifteen tubes of her own toothpaste."

"She once helped me rewrite an English paper four times."

"That's not particularly altruistic. I'm pretty sure she gets a kick out of rewriting things, both in her mind and on paper."

"She brings me out of myself," I added. "She's really taught me to let my hair down and try to let life happen instead of having to plan every single moment. Except for my classes, which she thinks I should plan to the smallest detail." I studied his hand against the console as I searched for the right words. "Camdyn encourages me to soar a little higher, and I keep her grounded. We're a good combination."

"That's a lovely speech. Admit it, though—she drives you a little insane, right?"

My heart lurched inside my chest, because I wanted to like Charlie, but I really didn't want to hear him say anything disparaging about my best friend.

"She's really a phenomenal person, you know? I guess from your viewpoint she might be your annoying sister, but I thank God every day for her. If I had a sister, I'd want her to be Camdyn."

I dared to let my eyes linger on him, and he rewarded me with a breathtaking smile. "Perfect answer. I was just testing you."

"Why?"

"To see if you're as great as Camdyn says you are. So far, you're living up to your reputation."

"Oh." Turning back to the window, I tried to hide the impact of his words. Camdyn's brother was most definitely getting under my skin, in the best of ways.

"Camdyn's an awesome sister, and I wouldn't trade her for a million bucks," he continued. "Just don't tell her I said that. It would ruin all the fun we have teasing each other."

He pulled the car into the parking lot of a shopping mall, locating a parking spot quite a distance from the doors. As he stilled the engine, I pushed open my door, drawing a deep breath of the cold winter air. Within seconds he was standing next to me. When I realized I was thinking about taking his hand, I forced my fingers into my pockets. A car whizzed past on my left, and he reached out and looped my hand into the crook of his arm.

"Just looking out for you," he insisted, pausing a second with his fingers against mine on his arm. Drawing my focus to the mall, I began walking beside him.

"Tell me about your baseball obsession," I suggested, bringing myself slightly closer to his side as I walked.

"I wouldn't call it an obsession."

"Your bedroom and your wardrobe would beg to differ."

"Ouch. I guess I do really like baseball. I have as long as I can remember."

"But you didn't play?"

50

"I really wanted to, but I wasn't any good." He chuckled as he shook his head. "Really no good, to the point that the coach actually asked me to stop trying out for the team because he felt sorry for me."

"That had to hurt."

"A little. The truth is, I've always felt like baseball was supposed to be part of my life."

He didn't elaborate as we stepped through the sliding glass doors and into the warmth of the mall, but I couldn't let that statement go unexplained.

"Supposed to be part of your life?"

"Yeah." He drew to a halt in front of a pretzel stand, turning toward me. "This might sound a little crazy, but baseball is the only thing I remember about my dad. I had this small, worn brown glove, and he was really patient with me. I can still see his face as he tossed the ball to me, his eyebrows lifting with every flip of his wrist. It always stuck with me, I guess, because it's the only memory I have of him. Do you think it's odd?"

"No, not odd. I think that's lovely."

He nodded his head slightly as a hint of a smile curved up the corners of his lips. "Good." He began walking again, and I self-consciously pulled my hand away from his arm. "The truth is, when I think about being a dad myself someday, that's what I see. Me standing out in the yard, a small tyke with a mess of blond hair, and a little brown baseball glove."

"That's beautiful."

"*You're* beautiful." He shoved his hands in his pockets as he tilted his head toward a storefront. "I guess I shouldn't say so, though. I'll try to keep my thoughts to myself."

Charlie stepped inside a trendy shop and began perusing clothing racks rather absently, not really focusing on anything, and I fought the urge to look at him by peering at a nearby display of jewelry.

"So, what does the doctor do for fun, in his spare time?" I made sure to ask the question loud enough for him to hear, but didn't dare look at him with the incriminating smile on my face.

"I study a lot, actually."

"That leaves no doubt you're Camdyn's brother."

I turned to see him motioning toward the door, so I quickly stepped up behind him, following him back into the crowds.

"I'm sure I don't study like she does. She's always had her head in a book for as long as I can remember. But I definitely want to get my money's worth, and I want to be good at my job when the time comes." He paused to glance in my direction. "And I'm glad you're acknowledging the whole doctor thing. Not that it really matters, but since you put so much emphasis on it..."

"That was mostly a joke. Just because you imagine something doesn't make it any more likely to become reality. A couple days ago, Camdyn was imagining herself as a Chinese peasant or something. She said she was fighting the Comintane or something like that."

"The Comintane?"

"You know Camdyn and her big words. I have no idea what she was talking about." For a second I felt slightly ridiculous, but his deep laugh allowed me to take a quick breath and let out a giggle myself.

We strolled past a storefront with a variety of keepsakes in the window, and a snow globe immediately caught my eye. The cozy home nestled inside held a dusting of snow on the roofline, and the trees nearby held their own smatterings of snow. It reminded me of home, back in Cape Girardeau. The home that now belonged to Mr. and Mrs. Pan, an elderly couple who would not be sliding around on their socked feet. Not related to Peter Pan, either—I asked, and they did *not* think my question was amusing. Just trying to lighten the atmosphere, since they were ripping out my heart.

"Found something?" Charlie asked, causing me to jump.

"No, just looking at this snow globe. It reminds me of home. I mean, the home I grew up in back in Cape Girardeau."

"You miss being there for Christmas?"

"Yes and no. My parents sold the house a couple years ago and moved to Nebraska, so I couldn't go home if I wanted to."

"I'm sorry."

"Don't be. If I went home, I wouldn't be here right now, and I'm having a good time, believe it or not."

He took a step closer and put his hand on my shoulder as he looked at the snow globe. "You know, when you're not being completely honest, your eyes change color."

"What?" My breath caught in my throat as I stared at his profile.

"Yeah, they change to a slightly darker color of brown, like the difference between regular coffee and the stuff I brew when I'm cramming for a test."

"What exactly are you accusing me of lying about?"

"Who said you were lying?" he asked, facing me. "You had that look in your eyes when you were pushing around the cereal in your bowl this morning, and earlier when you were talking about Ash, like you're hiding something. Just now, you said not to be sorry about you being here, but I can tell it bothers you."

"A little." I glanced away lest he see anything else in my eyes that I would rather keep to myself.

"Because you feel like you went away to college, and your home disappeared?"

"Something like that." I pretended to look at the other items behind the glass. "You know, you're probably right. I should be honest about Ash."

"And?" His tentative tone made my heart skip a beat.

"I'm not sure why Camdyn told you that, but I haven't dated a football player since high school. I don't know anybody named Ash, except a girl named Ashley who lives in our dorm. And I definitely don't have a boyfriend."

He chuckled as he reached a hand up to the back of his neck, shaking his head. "Nicely played, Cammie. What a bratty little sister move."

"Why would she lie about that?"

"Oh, I know exactly why," he muttered. "I saw that picture on the dresser, and I said, 'Wow, you didn't tell me Trina was a knockout.' She said, 'Off limits, Charlie. Anyway, she has a boyfriend.'"

"That's really what happened?"

"God's honest truth. But you and I have talked on the phone a few times, so I feel like we're over the first hurdle."

"Oh?"

He smiled, turning my stomach inside out. "Yeah, and I came home early hoping I'd get to spend some time with you."

"You're messing with me." I fell into step beside him as he began moving through the throngs of people.

"Nope." I felt the tips of his fingers tickle across the palm of my hand right before his fingers laced through mine. "The truth is, I bought Camdyn a present a couple weeks ago. But I'll probably be shopping for Camdyn's present a few more hours, at least. For your sake, of course, since you need a present."

"Yeah, about that. I bought her present a couple months ago."

"So you came along just to be with me." He rewarded me with a smile as his thumb rubbed along mine where our hands were linked together.

"Pretty much. Does that make me a bad friend?"

"The worst, but I'll give you a pass." He stopped in the midst of the crowd of people, turning to grin at me. "So, how are we going to keep this a secret?"

Chapter Six

Three hours we spent "shopping" for Camdyn before Charlie suggested we return to the house, in case they got suspicious. Judging by the look Willa gave me when we came through the door, the suspicions were already floating around. Strangely enough, though, they hadn't seemed to make it to the one who might have protested. Her perceptiveness when it came to my feelings was definitely hindered in that setting.

To be perfectly honest, I felt mildly guilty. Just when I would begin thinking about coming clean and spilling the beans about Charlie, he'd catch my eye across the room and I'd feel my heart start pounding again. He was pretty much the perfect catch: Loved his sister and his grandma, was studying for a successful career, and wanted his own family someday. He even had a perfectly good, sigh-worthy excuse for his weird baseball obsession.

Yeah, Charlie Taylor was definitely dangerous in the best possible ways.

So, instead of dwelling on the possibilities or the guilty feelings, I offered to help Willa make dinner. She patiently showed me how to make meatloaf and twice-baked potatoes, and while the meatloaf was baking, she led me through making homemade icing to go with Charlie's birthday cake. She even showed me the secret box where she kept her handwritten recipes, explaining that those were to go to Charlie someday. Most everything sentimental she figured Camdyn would want, but she didn't want the recipes to go to waste. When I couldn't hold back a laugh at that tidbit, she gave me a conspiratorial smile and glanced into the living room. Camdyn had draped her legs over the back of the couch with her curls hanging over the armrest, a book five inches in front of her face.

"My Camdyn will change the world someday, but it won't be through cooking," Willa whispered, patting me on the shoulder. "At least I hope not, because I wouldn't want her to wind up in prison."

We sat down to dinner, the four of us, where Willa promptly began bragging about how I had cooked the meal with no assistance. That wasn't entirely true, but I didn't correct her. Besides, with Charlie's leg touching mine under the table, I didn't have the nerve to say much of anything, lest I become obvious and let the proverbial cat out of the bag.

After dinner, Willa brought out Charlie's cake and Camdyn sang off-key as he cringed. When Willa retreated to the living room to prepare us for a Charlie Brown evening, I watched in fascination as they all settled into their spots for the ritual. Camdyn plopped into the recliner, pulling a worn brown crocheted afghan over her. Willa planted herself in the glider, rocking back and forth. Charlie settled onto the couch, taking up the whole of the space with his long legs and his elbows behind his head. As I glanced around the room at the lack of seating options and prepared to lower myself onto the floor, Charlie pulled his legs back and sat up, relinquishing one of the couch cushions.

"It's my birthday, and you're forcing me to give up the couch," Charlie complained under his breath.

"As though you need an entire couch," Camdyn complained. "Trina, how did you put up with him while you were shopping today?"

"It was rough," I assured her, easing myself down next to Charlie.

"I treated her like part of the family," he said. "Be quiet, because the show's starting. I could really use a pillow."

"Go get a pillow then." Camdyn shifted her attention away from Charlie and focused instead on the television.

He stretched and leaned toward me, placing his head on my lap as he looked in the direction of the TV. My eyes widened, and I glanced at Willa, but her attention was elsewhere.

"Trina makes an excellent pillow," Charlie teased, causing Camdyn to look in our direction.

"Ugh, why do you have to be so weird? Just push him off the couch, Trina. You don't have to put up with that."

She failed to observe the fact that my fingers were brushing Charlie's shoulder, her brother's back was warm against my thigh, and my heart was effectively in my throat.

Charlie glanced up at me briefly, a clear signal to me that he had managed to enable physical contact between us while keeping his sister convinced that he was trying to be obnoxious. I shrugged my shoulders and gave Camdyn a defeated half-grin. She shook her head in disgust and went back to watching Lucy torment poor Charlie Brown.

Our own Charlie kept on tormenting me in his own way throughout the cartoon, occasionally reaching his hand up to drag a finger slowly down my arm, eyeing Camdyn to be certain she wasn't watching. It was a very bratty move, but my desire to keep our growing attraction under wraps won out over my instinct to swat him.

After the Peanuts gang sang the closing number, Camdyn and Willa announced they were going to bed, and Camdyn offered to let me crash in her room. I assured them I would be fine on the couch. Charlie complained about being tired and disappeared before either of the ladies could.

Slightly disappointed, I spread the sheets and blankets on the couch, lowered my head to the armrest, and stared at the ceiling, unable to sleep. A million thoughts began tumbling through my head, my mind refusing to calm. Were my parents sad that I wouldn't be sharing Christmas with them? Should I have faced my feelings instead of running to St. Louis? Was Charlie simply toying with me?

My eyes tried to focus on the small, blinking colored lights on the Christmas tree across the room. They began swimming together, so I forced my eyes closed, trying to fall asleep.

"Psst," I heard near my feet, and my eyes flew open, focusing on Charlie in his plaid pajama pants and navy-blue T-shirt. Sitting up, I nervously shoved my hair away from my face, drawing the blanket up to my chest.

"I know this is late notice, but I was wondering if you had plans this evening."

All thoughts of him toying with me flew to the wayside as I stared at his handsome face as he waited for my answer.

"What do you have in mind?"

"Oreos," he stated, producing the package of cookies from behind his back. "Maybe we could just talk?"

"You had me at Oreos," I told him, moving my feet from the couch so he could sit next to me.

♥

"I can't believe she never told me that story," Charlie said with a laugh, taking care to keep his voice quiet. "I bet she has all kinds of embarrassing stories that she's kept hidden, doesn't she? Come on, tell me another one."

"Hmm..." I bit my lip as I looked toward the ceiling briefly. "Oh, did she tell you about the movie incident?"

"You mean *Harry Potter*?"

"Um, no."

"*The Notebook*?"

"How many movie incidents can there be?"

"Apparently several. Please, continue."

"I think it was the first year we roomed together, pretty close to the holidays. She gets so worked up toward the end of the semester about her grades that she exhausts herself studying. Well, I really wanted to go watch *The Holiday*, you know...Jude Law, Kate Winslet, Jack Black."

"Irrelevant information," he whispered.

"I beg your pardon? I hardly think Jude Law is irrelevant."

"In this instance, maybe?"

"No, he's completely relevant. That's part of the reason I wanted to watch the movie. Anyway, she told me she was tired, but I still coerced her into going to the late showing. We were even on time for a change. She wore her sweatpants so she wouldn't be cold, and she never took her coat off. I guess she must have gotten all warm and toasty, because she dozed off."

"Nice."

"Yeah, except it gets worse."

"Camdyn's involved, so of course it gets worse."

"She got a little too comfortable while she was sleeping, and she kept leaning farther and farther toward the guy sitting next to us. Finally, he put his popcorn in the way to keep her from laying on him."

"She knocked the popcorn over?" he asked.

"Nope. She pretty much face-planted in it, and had no idea. I kind of poked her when the movie was over, and she just sat up like nothing happened. While we were walking out, people were giggling, and she asked very seriously, 'What's so funny? Did I miss the funny part?' I honestly couldn't give her an answer to that myself until we got out to the lobby and she turned to look at me."

"And?"

"Blonde curls covered in popcorn on one side of her face. She *looked* like she face-planted in it. It was so hilarious. But I was a good friend and tried not to laugh."

"I'll bet." He offered a charming smile as he glanced at the wall. "That clock says it's three in the morning. Do you think it's right?"

Returning his grin, I tilted my head to the side. "It's been right the rest of the day, so I'd guess it is now."

"It doesn't feel that late. You're pretty entertaining."

"So are you." He leveled his gaze on me, and I forced myself not to smile as I pressed my teeth into my bottom lip. "So, what happens on the 22nd? Since obviously the 21st and Charlie day is now gone."

"Sadly, that is a disappointing fact. On the 22nd, Grandma always goes to church to help prepare food. They have this big neighborhood-wide dinner on Christmas Eve, so it takes a lot of effort ahead of time. Tomorrow...or today, I guess, is mainly a work day. The 23rd is always fun, though, because we bless someone who can't repay us."

"Very cool," I whispered, grinning.

He continued to stare at me, so I focused on the tree again. The warmth of his fingertips trailed across the top of my hand, and I glanced down as he lifted my hand and looked at the palm, tracing his finger across it slowly.

"Did you know the human hand has 27 bones?"

It was such a random statement, I brought my other hand up to my lips to hide my smile. "No, I had no idea."

"And your heartbeat is triggered by electrical impulses," he continued, placing my palm flat against his chest. I'm pretty sure my heart rate climbed to an accelerated level simply due to that action, and he never took his eyes from my face.

"Fascinating," was all I managed to push from my lips.

"One to seven gallons of blood a minute," he said, holding my palm captive against his T-shirt. "That's how much your heart pumps, depending on what you're doing."

Even with his blue eyes focused so intently on my own, I fought the urge to giggle. "This is quite a biology lesson. Anything else you'd like to add?"

"There are **206** bones in the human body, and every single bone in *my* body is telling me to kiss you." Unsure how to respond, I simply raised my eyebrows. "And I just made it weird. I was trying to recite random facts so you would be reminded of the whole 'I'm a doctor' vibe I was going for. Now I can't even *try* to kiss you, because I ruined the moment."

"Maybe you can get it back," I suggested. "I can try to forget all that doctor stuff."

"No," he insisted, linking his fingers with mine and dragging my hand up to his lips slowly, never dropping eye contact as he kissed the back of my hand. "I'm only going to do it when it's perfect."

"Nothing's ever perfect." My words came out as a whisper, and he pressed his lips together as he nodded his head.

"True, but I have this theory."

"A theory," I repeated.

"Yeah, if I meet a girl I could imagine a future with, the first kiss has to be exactly right."

My head was spinning at his words, but I managed to keep myself composed. "Why is that?"

"Because if she winds up being the right girl, there's a chance it could be the last first kiss. I don't want to screw that up."

"No," I whispered.

"No, so I think it's probably best if I call it a night." Leaning toward me, he touched his lips gently to my cheek. "Good night."

"Good night," I answered, my cheek still burning from the spot his lips had touched. Snuggling into the covers, I rested my head against the couch, closing my eyes and trying to decide if I could imagine a future with Charlie Taylor.

Chapter Seven

"Willa, do you want these over here?" I asked, pointing to a platter she had piled high with homemade dinner rolls. We had been at the church for a couple hours preparing food, and it seemed like she was just getting started.

"No, honey, just take them over to that counter and someone will bag them." Stepping across the room, I waited as I saw Camdyn strolling toward me, nonchalantly glancing about.

"Where have you been, Cam?"

"Entertaining the kids. They always demand that I hang out with them. Grandma probably wishes they would leave me alone so she could get some more help with the food."

I had a sneaking suspicion that Willa was the one who suggested that Camdyn watch the kids, but I didn't voice my thoughts.

"There are a lot of guys here," I commented, glancing to my left where three or four twenty-something males congregated, loading boxes.

"Youth group guys from back in the day who are here with their parents." She had a twinkle in her eye as she focused on the little group. "Maybe you should go say hello, Trina. I know you didn't expect to meet any gentlemen on this trip, but it wouldn't hurt."

"I've sworn off meeting new people this Christmas." Ever since I met Charlie, that is. Yet another tidbit that I wasn't about to share with my best friend. "The dark-haired guy seems really interested in you, though. He can't keep his eyes off you, and he looks like a catch."

She only allowed a split second of study before she let out her breath in an exasperated sigh. "Be serious, Trina. The guy's wearing a Poison T-shirt. So lame."

"But it was totally okay for *me* to meet said guy a minute ago when *you* suggested it."

"I might have been a bit hasty in my suggestion. I apologize."

The aforementioned rocker began making a gradual move in our direction, so Camdyn responded by grabbing my hand and pulling me away from the other volunteers toward the empty sanctuary. The lights were off and only the last gleams of the day's sunlight filtered through the colored portions of the stained glass windows, illuminating

68

our steps. She sat in the fourth pew on the left and placed her elbows on the top of the pew in front of her.

"I don't know why I came in here," she whispered. "This room always makes me uneasy."

"Why is that?"

"This is where I was when I realized my mom was never coming back."

A cold chill skittered over me, and as I lowered myself next to her on the cushioned seat, I hesitated. She rarely ever mentioned her mother, and when she did, it was usually followed by a shake of her head and a vow not to talk about her again.

"How old were you?" I asked.

"Six. I don't remember the how or the why of the day, but I remember sitting in this exact spot, listening to a hushed prayer, and knowing that she was gone. It's funny— I don't even remember if I cared or it made me sad, I just remember the acknowledgement of the facts."

"I'm sorry."

"Don't be. She wasn't." She sniffed slightly as she stared ahead at the steps leading to the podium. "I always feel it worse here, though."

"Feel what?"

"Restlessness. I'm not even sure, really...a sense that I should belong somewhere. That I need to find home. But home is with Grandma, right? It's just a crazy feeling I have sometimes that makes no sense."

Shifting next to her, I placed my elbows on the pew by hers, resting my chin on my hands. "I think I understand. I can never go home again."

She glanced at me with an impish grin. "Don't be silly. I'm sure they're disappointed not to see you for Christmas, but they're not going to disown you or anything."

"I can go home to my parents," I corrected, folding my arms and laying my head on them. "Nebraska is waiting with open arms, but it's not home. Cape Girardeau is home, and I can't go back there. Nothing will ever be the same."

"It's exactly like that story I was writing in my head about the Kuomintang."

"Except I'm not a Chinese peasant woman, and I'm pretty sure no one in this room is planning a rebellion."

"Trina, I'm touched," she stated, giving a sarcastic grin. "You actually listened to some of my history talk, didn't you?"

"How could I not? You went on about it the whole drive to St. Louis."

"Sorry about that." She leaned back against the pew and wrapped her arms around her midsection. "Do you worry about summer at all? We're going to be unleashed on the world. I guess I'll come back here, but what about you? I hate the thought of you being in Nebraska alone, or wherever you decide to go."

Staring at the pattern of green splashed across the carpet from the reflection of the glass, I reached over and took her hand. "Let's make a promise that we'll never let the other one be alone. Sisters at heart. We'll always have each other."

"And you have me," Charlie added as he slid into the pew behind us, reaching his arms around both our shoulders.

"I'm not sure if that makes me feel better or worse," Camdyn said with a laugh. "Right, Trina?"

But I couldn't answer, because the truth was that it made me feel infinitely better.

"Camdyn?" A middle-aged woman stepped into the entryway, peering into the relative darkness. "Oh, there you are. The kids are looking for you."

"Duty calls." She rose to her feet. "Be nice to Trina, Charlie."

"You don't need to worry about me," he insisted as she stepped away from us. Leaning forward, he rested his chin on his arms next to my shoulder. "You're a pretty good friend, you know that? She's lucky to have you."

"I feel a little guilty keeping secrets from her."

"What sort of secrets?"

"Charlie secrets." Glancing at him, I fought the urge to grin.

"Probably best not to get her worked up." Staring at the front of the sanctuary, he let out a sigh. "What were you two talking about?"

"Your mother."

"Oh." He rose to stand behind me, and for a moment I worried that he would leave the room. Instead, he stepped around the side of the pew and settled beside me, weaving his fingers through mine against the velvety blue cushion beneath us. "She talk about her a lot?"

"Hardly ever." His hand was warm against my own, but I tried not to look at him. We were alone, and I didn't want to chance him thinking it was the perfect moment to share a first kiss. The dark church sanctuary just felt too thirteen-year-old schoolgirl to me.

"She probably doesn't remember her. I barely do."

"What do you remember?" My voice sounded quiet in my own ears, and as I glanced at him, his gaze drifted far away.

"About my mom? I remember she was at Dad's funeral. She didn't cry."

It felt as though my heart plunged a few inches in my chest, and I sensed tears pricking the corners of my eyes at his bluntness.

"That's terrible," I managed to breathe.

72

Turning toward me, he shook his head. "No, it made it easier. God blessed us by placing us with Grandma. Sure, I wish I had more time with my dad, but we had pretty stellar childhoods. I couldn't have asked for much better."

"Camdyn really looks up to you," I added, squeezing his hand.

"I know." A mischievous grin spread across his face. "That's why I can't believe you, instigating all this sneaking around. She's going to be so disappointed."

Chapter Eight

"If you're going to be a sissy about it, you can always stay here." Camdyn turned to look at me, mascara wand firmly in hand with what looked like a mad swarm of angry black caterpillars fighting under her eye. For a brief moment I considered telling her that Charlie might have a better method for applying under-eye black, since he loved baseball so much, but instead I chose to let her look like a complete nut.

"Nobody's being a sissy, and there's no need to start name-calling. I'm simply saying that I don't understand why blessing someone who can't repay you translates into dressing like a ninja."

"Trust me, a disguise is necessary." Twisting back toward the mirror, she proceeded to drag the mascara wand under her other eye until both cheeks were streaked with the black stain. "You're welcome to stay here and take a nap. I've never seen you be so tired."

A protest rose in my throat, but I swallowed it. Camdyn and I had done a bit of shopping early in the morning, and then I came home and slept on the couch for a few hours. From her vantage point it probably did seem a bit lazy on my part, but I couldn't tell her I had been up until the wee hours of the morning two nights in a row talking to her brother.

"I'm wearing head-to-toe black, is that not enough for you?" I asked. "I feel like I've stepped into an episode of *The Twilight Zone* or something."

"Nice, Cammie," I heard Charlie's voice behind me, the tone immediately causing my heart to race. "You look like a clown."

The way she brandished that mascara wand, I believed she might use it to run him through. Her surly look only lasted a moment, though, before she gave him a smirking grin.

"You're just not used to having to cover up angelic good looks like Trina and me, Charlie. One sight of our faces is bound to blow your cover."

"If you blow my cover, it would be because of whatever you tripped over, not your heavenly good looks. Speaking of which, Trina, you look good in black. Dangerous, even."

Normally I wasn't given to blushing, but whether or not the physiological reaction was visible on my face, I felt the heat creep into my cheeks.

"You're such a goofball," Camdyn muttered, pulling a black stocking cap over her blonde curls, doing her best to stuff her hair inside.

"Are we ready?" Willa asked from the hallway. Turning, my eyes widened as I witnessed Camdyn's grandmother also dressed in black, with a perky little pillbox hat atop her head, complete with black net veil draped over the front. "It never hurts to be fashionably sneaky," she informed me with a quick wink.

Suddenly I didn't feel quite as ridiculous in my black sweatshirt and yoga pants that Camdyn loaned me.

♥

"Positions," Willa ordered as she brought the dark-gray sedan to a stop in front of a slim two-story house with one solitary strand of Christmas lights hanging over the window.

"What is she talking about?" I asked Camdyn, seated next to me in the backseat.

"Drop and dash," Charlie informed me, turning around to face us from his "shotgun" position. He and Camdyn had both shouted the word as soon as Willa locked the front door of the house, but he was a split second faster. I was rather glad, because sitting in the back of the car with Charlie didn't seem like a good idea.

"The family didn't have money for Christmas, so we bought the kids a couple toys," Willa explained. "The challenge is dropping the gifts by without being seen."

"So you ring the doorbell and scatter?" Suddenly the black clothing was making some sense.

"We haven't been caught yet," Camdyn added beside me.

Glancing again at the house, I couldn't stop a puzzled expression from showing on my face. "Won't they see the car in front of the house?"

Willa nodded with a smile as she glanced in the rearview mirror. "They would, which is why we're parked three houses away."

"Got the goods?" Camdyn said.

"Right here," Charlie answered. "Number 14. You ready?"

Just like that, it was almost like I was watching a break-in on television. Willa was waiting in the car while three people clad in black were slinking down the street, stealing across the yard, and standing in front of a run-down replica of the house we had parked near a moment before. The fact that I was involved in the trio of sneaks left me feeling liberatingly excited.

"Escape plan," Camdyn whispered to her brother.

"What do you mean, escape plan?" I interrupted. "Don't you just run?"

"You trust Camdyn to simply run back to the car?" Charlie's face had the appearance of raising his eyebrows, although I couldn't see them under his stocking cap. "Here's the plan. You girls wait by the side of the house. As soon as I ring the doorbell, make your way behind that brown van in the driveway. Got it?"

"Got it." Taking me by the hand, Camdyn pulled me toward the edge of the house. Listening intently, I waited for the sound of the bell, but knew it was too muffled to hear when Charlie began sprinting toward us. Jerking Camdyn backward, I half-dragged her toward that van. We stopped next to the mirror on the driver's side right as Charlie drew up beside us, placing a finger to his lips to keep us quiet. Turning, I peered through the windows in the van to the other side, where I could see the front porch.

A light came on, and then a young man stepped outside, looking from one side of the yard to the other before he stooped to lift the bag. Had he not flipped on the light, he might have seen us, but the glow around him allowed us to blend into the dark.

As he reentered the house, we slowly backed away, careful to remain out of view as we crossed two more yards in our return to Willa's car.

"Success?" Willa asked as we pulled open the car doors, still sitting at her post as the getaway driver.

"Yep," Charlie said. "Trina's a pro. I have to wonder if she does this sort of thing all the time."

I shook my head as he turned to look at me. Camdyn and I had admittedly done some ridiculous things on campus, but never sneaking onto someone's property. Unless you counted those sorority girls who thought they would beat us in a scavenger hunt. Or the time we were avoiding that guy from her American History class. Or that one episode when I thought Mike Adams was cheating on me.

But we never wore black in those instances, so they were totally different.

The car crept back onto the street, and I noticed that it took Willa a few seconds to turn on the headlights. She was taking this incognito thing very seriously.

"How long have you been doing this?" I wanted to know.

Willa glanced up at me in the rearview mirror again. "We started all the Christmas traditions the first year the kids and I were together on Christmas, but the stealthy gift giving we've only been doing for a little while. How long do you think it's been, Camdyn?"

"I was probably fourteen, because you let Charlie drive. It was one of the most horrifying nights of my life."

"Charlie wasn't the best driver," Willa admitted with a quiet laugh.

"We're lucky to be alive," Camdyn added. "They've never let me drive, strangely enough."

"You're lucky we let you come at all." Charlie glanced back at her to add emphasis to his snarky comment.

While we drove the few miles to the next stop, Willa told me that she began the traditions on each day as a way to bring their small family together that first year. She lost her husband and son very close together, and they all needed some brightening in their lives that holiday season. Willa's words made my silly complaints about seafood and weird step-cousin Todd feel immature, unwarranted, and selfish. Staring out the window, I suddenly felt guilty about not being with my parents.

♥

Willa pulled the car to the end of a long driveway and killed the headlights, adjusting her pillbox hat as though she were channeling the charm and grace of Audrey Hepburn. I had to smile to myself at Camdyn's quirky grandmother. Making her acquaintance had given me a lot of clarity regarding Camdyn and many different facets of her personality.

"Game plan?" Charlie asked.

"Keep Camdyn from screaming," I said.

"That tree branch grabbed me," she explained for the umpteenth time.

"And the air trips you and food spills itself on you." Even in the darkness, I could sense the teasing look on Charlie's face and hear it in his voice.

"Game plan?" Camdyn said, clearly attempting to steer the conversation away from her unfortunate incident at our second stop of the evening.

"The Websters' home burned down last month," Willa answered. "They're staying with her sister until they get on their feet, so they're in need of monetary help."

"So we have an envelope," Charlie completed. "Easy as pie, as long as nobody screams."

Camdyn answered his taunt by opening the car door and stepping out into the night. I followed by exiting on my side, where Charlie was quickly next to me. Together the three of us strode purposefully down the dark driveway, turning a bend and coming in view of the house. All of the trees seemed to be situated in our general vicinity, with the home itself placed on a large, almost vacant plot of land.

"Problem," Charlie whispered. "There's nowhere to hide."

"So we just ring the bell and run like the wind," Camdyn suggested. Easy for her to say. I was pretty sure "run like the wind" was not in my body's vocabulary.

"No way will we get away without them seeing us. We'll have to hide around the side of the house for a few minutes." Charlie began walking forward again, but Camdyn stayed put.

"Sounds like a disaster waiting to happen," she mumbled.

"With you involved...probably."

"Why don't you go, and we'll wait back at the car?" Camdyn suggested to her brother. "That way the chances of being caught will be way less."

Not getting caught sounded pretty good, but walking back to the car without the blond-headed guy in the black stocking cap didn't intrigue me at all.

"Go ahead, Cam, and I'll wait here to make sure Charlie gets back okay."

She shrugged her shoulders as she turned and strolled back toward the car, while I remained rooted in my spot. It was only while standing there, unmoving, that I realized how cold the wind was as it snuck its way inside my clothes on its trek past my body. A shiver swept over me.

"Cold?"

I had expected Charlie to head off toward the house since I stated I would be waiting, but when I turned he was mere inches from me, his hands finding their way to my shoulders. He began rubbing my arms in an effort to keep me warm.

"I'll be fine," I insisted, the warm, woodsy scent of his cologne drifting to me in the wind.

"Come with me. It'll be fine, I promise. There's a hedge row right in front of the house, so you can wait for me there to keep out of the wind until we hide." Giving me a hesitant smile, he tilted his head. "Or, you can go back to the car with Camdyn."

"And miss seeing the dangerous Charlie Taylor in action?" I teased through chattering teeth. "Not a chance."

Without a word, he took my hand and led me up the long driveway, pulling me close to him to block the wind. For a split second I hoped that Camdyn kept walking toward the car and hadn't changed her mind to follow us, but with the wind whipping around, the thought quickly carried off on the cold breeze.

"You want to wait around the side of the house?" he whispered as we neared the dark front door, my eyes focused on the dim light evident behind the curtains. The hedge row was low to the ground now that we were next to it, but being around the side of the dark house wasn't appealing either.

"Maybe in the hedges, like you suggested?"

Smiling, he gently nudged me toward the squatty row of bushes, while I began rethinking my decision. I consoled myself with the thought that there would likely be nothing hiding there in the cold.

Except myself, of course.

And then I prayed they didn't have a wild cat.

Inching my body behind the shrubs wasn't too difficult, but peering toward Charlie from my covert position was rather tricky. He hadn't really said what he would do once he rang the doorbell, but now that I was crouched behind the bushes, I had my doubts about whether I could quickly exit to run with him.

He turned to give me an enticing grin from his post on the porch, and although he probably couldn't see me from his vantage point, my heart skipped in my chest. By that point it was clear that I was attracted to him, but there was so much more to it. Never before had I met a guy like Charlie, content to sit on his grandmother's couch with me until the wee hours of the morning, never making a move toward anything other than sharing conversation.

At least, no attempts apart from the one misguided effort to woo me with the biology lesson. The mere reminder made me choke back a giggle.

Charlie stooped to place the envelope on the porch and then pressed the button, barely taking a step in my direction when the lock clicked and the door began to creak open. Eyes wide, he dove into the bushes, landing awkwardly next to me with his elbow pressed against my abdomen.

The porch light flicked on, and he pressed his index finger to my lips in an effort to remind me to be quiet. As though I needed a reminder. I wasn't Camdyn, with the propensity to scream at inopportune moments. No, I was the one who stared discomfort in the face and persevered.

Mostly, anyway. At the present moment, the only things keeping me stone-still were the facts that we were likely to be spotted at any moment, there were cold, sharp rocks beneath my thighs that were jutting into my pants, and I could feel Charlie's breath on my cheek.

An excruciating couple of hours went by as we sat there awkwardly in the middle of those bushes. Not really, but the seconds felt like they took forever, neither of us daring to move a centimeter, staring into each other's eyes. Finally, we heard a male voice make a comment that someone must have run off, calling into the house about the envelope as he turned off the porch light and closed the door.

"I think you dented my spleen," I whispered to Charlie as I tried to adjust to the dark. He pulled his elbow back, but didn't move the rest of his body.

"That's not your spleen, it's way higher than that. You're talking about your intestines."

"Stop abusing the situation, Dr. Taylor." I laughed quietly so he would know I was teasing. "Seriously, though, you're killing me here. Can you move a little?"

"No," he stated. I narrowed my eyes at him, watching his widen in return. "I'm being honest. Something has the back of my pants."

Unable to slide past him on those rocks, I reached both arms around his waist, lowering them until they reached the top of his jeans. As I ran my fingers across his waistband, I discovered that his belt loop had somehow hung on a twisted, stubby branch.

"Just for the record, I didn't plan this."

I dared a glance into his eyes as I tugged sideways on his belt loop. "Sure you didn't."

"Not that I wouldn't have, but there are too many variables. Convincing Cam to stay in the car and you to hide in the bushes, finding the exact section of this shrubbery that would stick to me like glue..."

"For someone who didn't plan it, you seem to have all the pieces of the puzzle memorized." One final jerk, and his entire body seemed to sink against me. "What do you call that?"

Pressing his right fist down onto the rocks, he shoved his body back a few inches as he drew his left hand upward, his index finger making its way to my lips again.

"Ssshh," he whispered as he lowered his face, gently sliding his hand around the back of my neck as his mouth descended to mine, surprisingly warm after our chilly hike. His kiss was leisurely and overwhelming, so deliciously slow that I could barely force myself to think. Even though it was unrushed, there was nothing timid or hesitant about it on either of our parts. Truth be told, I'd been dreaming about Charlie's kiss ever since the first time he mentioned it, wondering when and where his "perfect" moment would find me.

And now that he'd kissed me, I knew that he thought I was worthy of that first kiss—the one he'd been saving just in case it was the last. That fact made it that much sweeter.

His lips pulled away from mine as he trailed his finger over my mouth. "You taste like strawberries," he said. "I love strawberries."

I couldn't help but smile as he remained there, precariously holding himself above me.

"This is your perfect moment?" I teased softly. "Hiding in the bushes?"

"I'm pretty confident that it doesn't matter, as long as it's with the right girl." He dropped one more quick kiss to my lips before he went to one knee, peeking at the front porch as he stood. Stepping away from the rocks, he held out his hand so I could rise and join him. As I snuck across the rocks, I placed my hand in his, in case he wanted to offer another one of those kisses. My heart sank a little when he simply glanced toward the trees further up the driveway, determined to head in that direction.

Hand enclosed firmly in Charlie's, I was extremely aware of two things:

Number one—I had definitely fallen for my best friend's brother.

And number two—I would forevermore carry strawberry lip gloss in my pocket.

Chapter Nine

Whatever I thought Christmas Eve might look like at Camdyn's home, I certainly hadn't imagined exchanging secretive flirty glances with her brother every time I passed him in the house while I attempted to keep my pulse from racing. In order to keep myself busy, and my mind firmly off Charlie, I volunteered to help Willa in the kitchen while Camdyn finished her Christmas wrapping.

When dinner time finally arrived, I set out to find Camdyn, expecting to find her on the couch or stretched across her bed. After checking both those locations and coming up empty, I proceeded to the middle of the hallway and stood there, slightly confused.

"Camdyn?" I called. "Where are you?"

"Green Gables," was the muffled response. Stepping to her doorway again, I peered inside. When I couldn't locate her, I walked around the edge of the bed to find her lying on the floor, propped up by her elbows, completely engrossed in a book. It was impossible for me not to notice that she also had Christmas music playing in the background, and her feet were tapping a rhythm against her dresser.

"Dinner's ready." I attempted to withhold my grin as I stared at her, but she was just so endearingly quirky, one side of my mouth unwillingly traveled upward.

"I do believe she's right."

Crossing my arms against my chest, I stared down at her as she closed her book and flopped over, gazing up at me from her upside-down vantage point.

"She?"

"Anne Shirley."

Naturally, Anne Shirley. What had I expected, after all? Camdyn convinced me to read *Anne of Green Gables* once, and there was one line that stood out to me...along the idea that if you're going to imagine, it might as well be on something worth the effort. That pretty much fit Camdyn to a T.

"What did Anne Shirley say?"

After all this time, I really should know better than to goad her.

"It's easier to be good if you have fashionable clothes. I think I quite agree. Or at least a fabulous pair of shoes."

"You'll get no arguments from me."

Sitting up, she turned to face me, pulling one knee toward her chest.

"I do believe I could endure a whole closet full of unfashionable clothes for the honor of having the friendship of a kindred spirit like you, Trina Miller."

"You've gone nutty."

"Have I? Would you not give up fashionable clothes for the privilege of spending Christmas with my fantastic grandmother, rather than your weird step-cousin?"

"Actually, Todd's not seeming so weird right about now."

"You're my Diana Barry."

Uh huh. Anne's best friend? The kind of sane one that balances Anne out?

Yeah, it makes sense.

"You've gone off your rocker," I insisted with a giggle. "Come on, your grandma's waiting."

Camdyn rose and tossed the book on her bed, giving me an exaggerated kiss on the cheek before she walked out of the room. The only thing I could do was remain stationed there, solemnly shaking my head. By now I'd grown accustomed to her eccentricities, but she was such a puzzle. The fact that she managed to remain aloof and yet be looked at with admiration back at campus always baffled me, but here I stood in her bedroom feeling the same sort of weird connection that we'd had from the beginning.

I was totally her Diana Barry.

Or maybe she had finally sucked me into her delusions.

Shaking off those thoughts, I hurried out of the room and down the hall to the kitchen, where the small table was set with the evidence of Willa's efforts. She really was a fantastic cook, and I envied whoever would get to use her recipes with Charlie later.

As I settled at the table, Charlie was seated next to me almost instantly, grinning as he pressed his leg against mine under the table.

And just like that, thoughts about Camdyn and food and the future were tossed out of my mind, because the present was all about the man sitting next to me.

♥

Maybe it was because my parents never pushed Santa Claus, or perhaps because they didn't have a strong belief system to make Christmas special, but other than looking forward to the rather gluttonous day of endless dessert and a few fancy gifts, I didn't put much stock in the holiday. Not the way Camdyn's family did, anyway. My mother might have held parties at our home, but it was solely for the sake of socializing. There were no daily reminders of it being the Christmas season, no attempts to focus on thinking about the less fortunate, and definitely no sentimental trips down memory lane.

It really was like I had awakened inside that Charlie Brown story, where they were all making fun of him for having the scrawny tree, but he somehow helped the gang understand the real reason for the celebration in the first place. In the midst of an aluminum holiday landscape, Camdyn's family embraced the scrawny real tree, and I wasn't sure what to make of it.

That Christmas Eve, they didn't go to a grand party or sneak peeks at their gifts. Willa sat in her recliner in the living room with the lights dimmed, the glow of the Christmas tree blinking in the corner, and she read a passage out of her Bible. I couldn't know for sure, but since my own eyes were having trouble adjusting to the low light, I imagined that she had the entire thing memorized.

Listening to Willa tell the story with emotion in her voice, my eyes began to well up with tears, and I scolded myself a bit for it. My best friend had grown up without her parents, had to earn scholarships to attend college, and hardly ever went out socially because she didn't want to waste her grandma's money. When she did spend any cash, she used her "summer fund" that she earned while working at a theme park. I had no right to be jealous of Camdyn, but in that moment, I was.

I was jealous because their holiday seemed loving, and real, and...like family.

Willa leaned over to the coffee table and picked up a small red velvet sack that looked very much like Santa's bag, dropping three little boxes into her lap. Smiling, she waited as Charlie and Camdyn moved toward her and took their boxes, and then she turned toward me to explain.

"That first year, on Christmas Eve, we were having a bit of a hard time forgetting our heartaches, so we decided to focus instead on the wonderful things the year brought us. It became a yearly tradition. We write one thing on a slip of paper, place it in the box, and hang our hope on the tree and everything it represents." She tilted her head to the side as she watched my reaction. "We've always hung our hopes on Jesus in this house."

Placing her box on my lap, Camdyn plopped beside me on the couch. "Go ahead. Open it," she urged. Pressing the string at the top aside, I pulled up on the lid, waiting as the tiny hinge opened. Inside were several strips of paper, all curled into pretty twists. My mind immediately envisioned Camdyn twirling the paper around the end of her pencil each year.

Unwrapping one strip of paper, I smiled hesitantly at my friend before I began reading. "Camdyn Taylor, age nineteen. For my roommate Trina, who is exactly the lovely best friend I needed." Shaking my head, I fought the tears rising to the surface. "Oh, come on, that's not fair."

"It's not my fault you pulled that one out of the box," she argued. "They're not all about you."

Pushing my fingers back into the box, I wrapped the end of one twist around my pinky, slowly pulling it up. "Camdyn Taylor, age fourteen. Mrs. Brown's history class, because she let me write about ancient Egypt instead of the Bay of Pigs."

"I found that more interesting at the time." She giggled as she leaned back against the couch cushions. "Obviously I didn't have my priorities straight, being thankful about homework assignments."

That didn't seem all too different from the Camdyn I knew from college, but I kept that thought locked away inside my head while I dumped the contents of her box onto my lap. "Another?" I asked, smiling at her. The next paper I unwrapped was written in crayon, and was obviously a child's handwriting. "Camdyn Taylor, age six. Charlie sits with me on the bus." Glancing over at the man in question, I saw him watching me with interest. "That's so sweet, Charlie. You must have been a fantastic brother."

"I was clearly delusional," Camdyn interrupted. Charlie huffed a protest, and she shrugged her shoulders in defeat. "Okay, I admit—Charlie used to protect me when we were kids."

"It took her fifteen years to acknowledge that fact," he commented, shaking his head.

Glancing at my lap, I stealthily pulled open another piece of paper. This one was in a different handwriting — likely Willa's. *Camdyn Taylor, age four. Jesus loves me. And Grandma. And Charlie.* Twisting it closed quickly, I kept my eyes on my fingers, not wanting to read that one aloud. Age four would have been their first year together after the accident. Instead of prying further into Camdyn's memories, I swept them back into the box.

"Read one of yours, Charlie," I suggested, trying not to think about how sad that year must have been for them.

Rather than open his box, Charlie moved to the vacant spot beside me and settled next to me on the couch as he held the box by the string and dropped it onto my lap just as Camdyn had. Carefully lifting the lid, I dared to glance over at him, confident that Camdyn couldn't see the private smile we shared.

"Charlie Taylor, age seven," I read as I glanced at the paper. "Murray sleeps in my room."

"Dog," he quickly informed me. "Really good dog. He died the year I left for college."

"Every boy needs a good dog." Staring into the box, I noticed that Charlie's papers were neatly folded rather than twisted like Camdyn's. "Let's see, number two. Charlie

Taylor, age eleven. Went to two Cardinals games this summer. Lankford tossed me a foul ball."

"I still have it."

"I'm sure you do. I've seen your bedroom."

"What should I write this year?" Camdyn asked, interrupting the laugh I shared with Charlie.

"It's supposed to be a secret," Charlie stated, "until we open them next year. That's what makes it fun."

"I know." Camdyn sighed as she reached for the pen and slip of paper her grandma held in her hands. "What about Trina? We can't leave her out."

"The boxes proved impossible to find, but I was able to find this little container and I tied a cord to the top."

Surprised, I fully turned to look at Willa, who had a cylinder that looked a lot like a tiny mailbox. Once again I fought emotion as I thought about the lengths to which this family had included me in their traditions, and I was at a loss for words as I stared at the container.

"Here sweetie," Willa continued, holding the item toward me with a pen and paper. "You don't have to leave it here. You can take it home with you, if you want."

No way was I taking that home. Sentiment like that belonged in St. Louis with the Taylors, not in Nebraska with the Millers. My parents probably didn't even put out a Christmas tree in that cold, sterile house. The Christmas ornaments were probably in some corner of the house in a box, right next to my dad's dusty books.

Camdyn handed me the paper, and I eyed it curiously. A whole year to pin my hope on, so what should I choose? Staring at the blank space, I twisted my mouth to the side as I considered my words. Beside me, Charlie turned to the arm of the couch and began writing. As Camdyn rose and stepped to the kitchen table to neatly fill out her sentiments, I placed the pen against the paper on my leg.

Trina Miller, I wrote. *Age twenty-one. Grateful for a Christmas I'll never forget.*

Twisting the paper as Camdyn had, I slid it into the little mailbox and held it up by the string, loving how I felt like I belonged in the little group.

"Here." Charlie interrupted my thoughts, thrusting a folded paper in my direction. "Take this for me, will you? I'll be right back."

The second I had possession of his memento, he jumped up and disappeared down the hall. One glance in Willa's direction told me she was busy with her own thoughts, and my curiosity was getting the better of me. Attempting to keep my peek a secret, I barely spread the paper apart, my eyes darting to the words.

Charlie Taylor, age twenty-four. The Christmas that my sister's best friend stole my heart.

Quickly shoving the paper inside the box, I closed the lid and rose, crossing the room to the hallway where I paused at Charlie's open bedroom door. He stood next to his dresser with a baseball in his hands. I quietly rapped my knuckles on the door.

"Hey," he stated nonchalantly. "This is the foul ball I was talking about." He held it out toward me, but I didn't take it. Instead, I wrapped my arms around him, resting my head on his shoulder. After his momentary surprise, I felt the warmth of his arms against my back as he drew me closer.

"I really like your hair like that," he muttered. "Did you curl it?"

"What an odd thing to say." I held him a little tighter as his fingers raked through the back of my hair. "To think I care about my hair when you wrote something so unbelievably sweet."

"You weren't supposed to read that."

"You wanted me to."

"Even so..." His lips grazed my skin, touching my forehead and then the curve of my cheekbone. "What am I supposed to do with you? She's going to kill me."

"We'll break it to her gently," I whispered, pulling back so I could look at his blue eyes.

"Oh, man." He chuckled as he placed his forehead against mine. "I've been telling myself this is a bad idea from the first night when I pretended I didn't know you were in my room, but I can't seem to help myself."

My mouth dropped open in shock at his admission, but I recovered enough to gather my senses. "You don't have to tell her, you know." No way did I want him to agree to that plan, but I felt the need to throw it out there, if nothing more than a test.

"She won't wonder why I keep calling you?" He pulled his gaze away as he glanced at the door. "It's too late for that. Unless you don't want..."

His eyes returned to my face, scanning my own for an answer.

"I'm really not a fan of long distance relationships," I told him. He nodded his head, inching back slightly. "So...I'm very serious when I say I'm willing to give this a go."

He offered a mischievous smile as he wove a strand of my hair through his fingers. "I promise you won't regret it."

"What sort of promise is that? Is it one of those 'all 206 bones in my body' promises?"

Laughing softly, he shook his head. "No, more like a 'one heart' promise."

"Can we make it a 'two heart' promise?"

Rather than answer, he pulled me closer, sealing our deal with a rather hurried but thorough kiss that left me feeling breathless.

"Strawberries," he whispered. "I love that." Stepping back, he put some space between us as he held the baseball out to me again. "As I was saying before, this is my baseball."

"The infamous Lakeford baseball." Taking it from his fingers, I passed it between my hands.

"Lankford," he corrected with a roll of his eyes. "You are really going to have to work on your baseball knowledge."

"And you'll have to work on your fashion sense. Not every occasion is an excuse to wear a Cardinals T-shirt."

"I actually might be able to argue that point, but I'll concede." With a lazy smile, he leaned his backside against his dresser. "This is me making an effort."

Crossing to the dresser to place his baseball back in its place, I smiled as sweetly as I could. "Lankford. Made an effort." Stepping away, I backed toward the door. "I better go back out there. See you later?"

"No."

Pausing midstride, I remained by the foot of his bed. "No?"

"It's Christmas Eve. I can't go out there on Christmas Eve, it would ruin everything."

"Ruin everything?" The skepticism was clear in my voice, because I was having a hard time understanding his words.

"Stuff just happens between Christmas Eve and Christmas morning. I don't want to see how it happens or prevent it from happening by being in the way."

For a split second I bit the inside of my lip, wondering why he was being so strange, until understanding washed over me.

"Charlie Taylor," I said, "age twenty-four. Doesn't want to spoil the magic."

"Trina Miller, age irrelevant. Don't miss the magic. It's Christmas."

Taking a deep breath, I studied his face trying to lock it in my memory. "I won't," I whispered, backing toward the hall.

Before I could stop to think, I made my way to the couch, picked up that little box that held my scrap of paper about the Christmas I'd never forget, and I hung it on a mostly empty branch. Standing before the simple tree, I stared at it and thought about what Willa said it stood for, all my hopes planted in the proper place. An arm slid around my shoulders, and Camdyn hung her box on the branch beside mine, where they clinked together as they settled.

"Welcome to the Taylor family, Trina."

Chapter Ten

Christmas Eve as a child was always rather sleepless, thinking about the presents I could open in the morning. That Christmas Eve, at the Taylor home, I drifted off the instant my head hit the armrest of the couch. After several very late nights sharing stories, hopes, and dreams with Charlie, I was rather exhausted.

My sleep was interrupted soon, though, by a slight rattling noise that I realized pretty quickly was ornaments tinkling together on the tree. Opening my eyes to a squint, I focused on Willa bending low to the ground and placing packages under the tree. I attempted to quietly adjust myself, but the couch groaned in protest as I moved and alerted Willa to my motion.

"I'm sorry, honey," she whispered. "I didn't mean to wake you."

"It's okay." Raising myself to a seated position, I watched as she rearranged the packages and then began dropping things in the stockings that were pinned to the wall. One had been placed there for me. Although it didn't quite match the others, I could tell she tried to find one that looked similar, just like she had with the box for the special memory. It was such a slight difference, it made me think about what life would be like as part of the Taylor family. I would be the one who didn't quite fit, but was close enough that they embraced me anyway.

"My presents were always under the tree the whole time, but I never believed in Santa anyway."

Why I felt I needed to offer that information was a puzzle, but she rose from her position and moved to the couch, sitting beside me.

"I'm not sure the kids ever believed in Santa, but there was something special about seeing their eyes light up on Christmas morning." Willa leaned her head back against the couch, her curls fanning about her face. It was the only feature Camdyn and her grandmother shared— those rather unruly curls. She closed her eyes, and I imagined her going back to some memory, watching as a smile turned up the corners of her lips. Nearly every wrinkle on her lovely face framed the corners of her eyes or the sides of her mouth, confirming to me that Willa made a point of smiling often. Not that I needed the visual clue, exactly. There was an unmistakable happiness in her home that was starting to settle itself deep inside me as well.

"You've done a great job," I finally said. "Everything about Christmas here is magical. Thanks for letting me share it with you."

"There's no magic, sweetie." Opening her eyes, she turned toward me as she placed her long, cool fingers over mine. "Cold hands, warm heart, my mom used to say." Smiling at her own memory, she let out a slight sigh. "I've always figured that God gives us things so we can share them with others. When I went through the most unspeakable heartache, He gave me joy. That's the contribution I can make. Some people have great talent, or a passion to change things, or the resources to impact groups of people. I have joy."

She didn't add anything else, and I felt like whatever I could say would be inadequate, so I just sat there beside her, her hand over mine as I stared at the newly filled stockings on the wall. My mind drifted back to the Christmas tree covered with the trendy silver ornaments back in Cape Girardeau, all the packages perfectly trimmed with bows and in identical paper. Nothing like the many different colors underneath this tree, but there were many good memories. Was my mom sneaking around after I went to bed? No, but she tried in her own way.

In fact, it was hard for me not to feel a little sorry for her now, imagining her with Aunt Shelly eating some kind of sea bass instead of turkey the next day.

Patting my hand, Willa rose from the couch. "I'm glad you're here, Trina. You've been a good friend to Camdyn." Her words brought a smile to my face. Stepping toward the hall, she paused to look back with a rather sly grin. "And for what it's worth, I think you're good for Charlie, too. Good night, honey."

♥

The night air stung my cheeks almost instantly when I stepped onto the back deck, and I pulled the pink fuzzy robe Willa had loaned me a bit closer. She thought I might want it since I had to sleep on the couch. I figured she imagined me sleeping there in a nightgown or something and thought I would want to keep Charlie from seeing my sleepwear. Since I wore lounge pants and a T-shirt, it didn't seem necessary.

Still, since it was protecting me from the chill, I was glad to have it. My fingers reached into the pocket, fiddling with the tube of lip gloss resting there. Immediately I felt rather idiotic, both for keeping the lip gloss in my pocket in the first place, and for the possibility in the back of my mind that Charlie might stumble upon me. He had most likely passed out upon hitting the pillow as I had done before.

Looking at the screen on my phone, I settled on the steps of the back deck, listening to the ringing on the other end. It dawned on me that I shouldn't be calling so late, but as I was rethinking my decision, a familiar voice sounded on the other end of the phone.

"Trina?"

Swallowing my hesitation, I tried to ignore the tears that immediately gathered in my eyes. "Hi, Mom."

"Has something happened?"

"No, not at all. I'm sorry to call you so late."

"It's okay, we were just wrapping up a game of bridge."

"Oh." I rolled the tube of lip gloss between my fingers and stared at it a moment. "Merry Christmas. That's really all I wanted to say. I'm sorry I didn't come home, and—"

"No, I'm the one who's sorry, Trina. I should have tried to have Christmas back in Nebraska. The house just isn't the same, though. I miss..."

"Home."

She paused after I said the word aloud, and it made me wonder if I had jumped the gun in finishing her sentence.

"Home," she finally agreed. "I miss home."

We both remained silent, and I assumed her mind was back in Cape Girardeau just like mine, staring at the Christmas tree across from the fireplace.

In my memory, Dad was in his study, intently going over his research, and I held a mug of hot cocoa in my hands. Mom placed a peppermint stick in my drink, and I secretly hated the taste of it screwing up my chocolate, but I adored the way it looked poking out of the mug. She had taken off her makeup after the holiday festivities, and had a mask around her eyes with a strange sea foam green tint. There were little chunks in it...of what I was afraid to ask. Bananas? Avocados? Likely whatever fad her social circle was praising at the time.

She leaned back against the couch and smiled toward the ceiling at nothing in particular. The sweet memory caused me to smile in the present.

"I love you, Mom."

She sniffed on the other end of the phone. "And I love you."

My toes began to sting from the cold, and I leaned forward, wrapping the ends of the bathrobe around them.

"When you're back from Florida, I'll go to Nebraska. Maybe we can mess the house up a little. Ooh, we could paint the kitchen yellow."

"Yellow, Trina?"

"Why not yellow?" Shivering slightly, I tugged again on the ends of the robe, trying to make it bigger. "Yellow is cheery and sunny. It would spread a little joy."

She laughed on the other end of the line as though I'd lost my marbles. "Sure, yellow. It's worth a shot."

"Tell Dad I said hello, and good night."

"Good night, sweetie," she told me as I hurried back into the house. Pressing the door closed with only the sound of a click, I shrugged out of the bathrobe and draped it over the back of the couch. Sitting down in the spot Willa had occupied not long before, I thought about her words.

When I went through the most unspeakable heartache, He gave me joy.

I peered across the living room at those two boxes Camdyn and I had hung together, resting side-by-side where they touched, as if they were destined to be a pair. Charlie's box was near the top—where I'd seen him hang it before he went to bed. That left only Willa's, near the center of the tree, shoved deep inside like she didn't want it to have a chance of slipping from its branch.

Unable to resist, I crossed the room and pulled it from its hiding spot, carefully lifting the lid. Although the room was dark, the gentle twinkling lights on the Christmas tree were enough to see at a close distance. Holding a little strip of paper next to a red bulb, I looked intently at the writing.

Willa Taylor, age seventy-six. Charlie and Camdyn.

My eyes darted to the hallway, feeling every inch like an intruder prying into her private life, but I couldn't stem my curiosity. Lifting out another paper, I tilted it toward the tree so I could catch the light.

Willa Taylor, age fifty-four. Charlie and Camdyn.

By that point, I was fairly certain the pattern would continue, but I withdrew one more sample just to be sure.

Willa Taylor, age sixty-three. Charlie and Camdyn.

Replacing the lid, I returned the box to its hiding spot, gently dragging my own away from Camdyn's. Retrieving a pen from the coffee table drawer next to the couch, I unwrapped the paper I had lodged inside earlier, staring at my statement. It was still very much true, being grateful for a Christmas I would never forget. I'd realized there was so much more, though.

Setting the pen on the paper, I scribbled a few more words.

For joy wherever you find it.

Chapter Eleven

$\mathcal{B}$ack home in Cape Girardeau, I usually woke on Christmas morning at around seven or eight to the scent of a breakfast casserole and the sounds of Vivaldi drifting through the vents. My dad was never a great lover of music, but on Christmas morning he liked the sound of violins.

At the Taylor home in St. Louis, Christmas morning amounted to being pounced on by a half-crazed lunatic at five-thirty in the morning. She was used to getting up at that time, no one should sleep in on Christmas, and *how exactly can you sleep at a time like this anyway?*

It immediately occurred to me that something very similar happened on one of those *Anne of Green Gables* movies, and it didn't work out so well for the heroine...in the beginning at least. Things always worked out well for her in the end, because it paid to be quirky and smart and have a great imagination.

"I don't know why I wake up so early," she said as she settled beside me. "Nothing I do ever makes Charlie get up. Ever. He'll just saunter out here when he feels like he's good and ready."

That tidbit of information might have caused her some irritation, but it was great news for me, because it meant I might have time to make myself presentable. By presentable, of course, that meant giving my hair a slight curl since he seemed to like it the night before, and making sure my lip gloss was expertly applied. It was shameless, really.

By the time I wandered into the kitchen, Willa was sitting there with a cup of coffee and Camdyn was across from her, chin on her hand and drumming her fingers on the table. When she locked eyes on me, she sat up straighter and narrowed her eyes.

"Um, it's Christmas morning," Camdyn informed me. "You're supposed to make a messy appearance in your pajamas as per tradition. We're not going to Glamour Shots."

"Oh." Thinking fast, I pulled out the chair closest to Willa. "We always dress up at my parents' house. Sorry."

It wasn't one hundred percent accurate, but if Charlie Taylor had been at my parents' house, you can bet I would have dressed up.

"Morning." Charlie's voice broke into my thoughts as he entered the room, grabbing a mug from the counter and heading toward the coffee pot. In the place of his standard uniform of Cardinals T-shirts, he decided to grace us with his presence that morning wearing a metallic gray button-up shirt that he had tucked into his jeans.

"Looks like I didn't get the memo," Camdyn complained. "Were you all planning a family photo or something and didn't bother to tell me?"

"What's that supposed to mean?" Charlie lifted the mug to his lips as he stared at his sister, but I knew exactly what she meant. If nothing else happened on that entire Christmas Day, seeing him dressed up just to make a point to me was more than enough.

Besides, he looked pretty spectacular.

"Are you wearing cologne?" Camdyn scoffed as she adjusted the topknot at the back of her head, hair sticking out every which way.

"I took a shower. It's not a crime." Giving his sister one last little teasing glare over his coffee, he pressed a kiss against Willa's cheek. "Merry Christmas, Grandma."

"Stop with the formalities," Camdyn ordered. "I want to see these awesome presents you got me that you had to sneak away for."

She popped up out of her chair like she was a bundle of energy while Willa stifled a yawn as she glanced at me. Of everyone else in the room, she and I were the only ones who had inside information on the magic, but even though I knew the secrets, it was still sucking me in a bit.

There was nothing at all posh and dignified about that Christmas morning. Willa was laughing even before the festivities started. Camdyn mouthed something at Charlie, and he turned around and threw something at her, after which they both smiled. Charlie then promptly lost something beneath the piles of paper, and what ensued was about five minutes of Camdyn standing on the couch while he ordered everyone else not to move. When she finally sat down, it was too far to the side of the armrest and she toppled over and ended up on the floor.

In the midst of all the silliness, I noticed Willa watching me. When she raised her eyebrows in my direction, all I could do was nod. She was right. Her efforts had been worth it, and it was impossible not to be caught up in their happiness.

Sitting on my corner of the couch, I stared at the gifts I had already opened from Willa and Camdyn, feeling every bit as loved as I was at my own home. Then, my eyes darted to the box next to them in the St. Louis Cardinals wrapping paper. My intention wasn't to save Charlie's gift for last, but I found myself doing it anyway. I glanced his way as I began to pull back the paper, but he was avoiding my gaze, so I stared at my lap while I uncovered the box. Carefully plucking it open, I pressed back the packing material to pull out the snow globe I had seen that day at the mall when Charlie and I were shopping. There inside that glass ball stood the likeness of my home in Cape Girardeau.

Holding the globe gently between my hands, I lifted my eyes again, catching Charlie's gaze focused on me. "Thank you," I mouthed, meeting his intense look and not bothering to avert my eyes. Without breaking our connection, he started tearing into his own present...one that I had purchased on the sly when I was with Camdyn.

Charlie's gaze finally dropped to his lap, and as the child-size baseball glove emerged from the paper, he sat unmoving. His sudden stillness caught the attention of Camdyn, to my complete dread, and in my head I sensed the questions coming.

What's going on?

Why did you get Charlie a kid's gift?

Why are you and Charlie buying gifts for each other anyway?

Then my heart sank when he still didn't look up. I had hoped it would remind him of his memories with his dad and why he loved baseball so much, but what if I offended him somehow? What if that was something he liked to keep to himself?

His full attention shot to me, and for a split second, I thought maybe I should say something. Before I had a chance, he shifted to one knee, stood up and walked toward me. I rose from my position on the couch like I was waiting...for what? I had no idea, but something.

The instant Charlie stood in front of me, his arms crept around my waist, pulling me into a hug. I was so thrilled that he was pleased, all I could do was throw my arms around his neck and hang on tight. It must not have been close enough, because he drew me even closer until my feet actually lifted off the ground. I laughed as he spun me around before he released me. No words passed between us as he smiled down at me, and that was perfectly fine. I knew exactly what he was saying.

"Am I missing something?" Camdyn blurted. Peeling my gaze away from Charlie, I managed to fix it on my wide-eyed friend who still sat on the couch, mouth gaping as she stared at her brother. "Are you and Charlie...?"

My brain ordered me to tell her something, anything, but instead I glanced at Charlie. That alone must have been enough of an answer, because she let out one of the most horrific, terrible groaning noises I've heard in all my life.

"Thank you so much, really. I don't even know what else to say." Crumpling the nearest wrapping paper into a ball, she threw it at us, hitting Charlie square in the arm. "Can you believe this, Grandma? Honestly?"

Camdyn turned her attention to Willa, who merely smiled and shrugged her shoulders.

"Well, that's it then," Camdyn stated, wrapping her arms across her chest as she stared emptily at the vacant area under the Christmas tree. "I hope you're all happy. It's officially the worst Christmas in the history of Christmases."

Epilogue

Three Years Later...

The last strains of the song began to fade away, accompanied by subtle clapping as Charlie took my hand, drawing it up to his lips and pressing a quick kiss to my knuckles. There had been many moments preserved in my memory relating to this man, but that one in particular had to rank right up there with the best of them. We had danced before many times, but this was the first time I had ever danced with Charlie as my husband.

"There's a perfect smile," he stated as he moved my chair so I could adjust the layers of white billowing around my feet. Pulling out the chair next to me, he settled into it as he rewarded me with a slow grin. "What are you thinking about?"

"Just thinking it's perfect that the kids at the daycare call me Miss Trina, because now they won't have to remember a new name." Glancing out at the room full of our friends and family, I allowed my focus to rest on Camdyn. "What are you thinking about?"

121

"I wish Grandma could have been here."

Instinctively I placed my hand on his arm, the fabric of the shirt under the tux jacket causing my fingers to slide slightly. "Me too," I whispered. "She would have been so proud of you, Charlie."

"She thought the world of you. I think she'd like the fact that you'll be in her house, using her recipes, keeping an eye on me."

"I can't say that I'll mind any of that myself. What about her, though?"

Charlie followed my line of vision to his sister, who was in animated conversation with my father. No doubt she'd found some academic theory he would speak about for hours, and she just wanted to show him that she could hold her own.

"Did you miss that part of the vows?" Charlie asked. "'I, Trina, promise to love, honor, and cherish Charlie as long as we both shall live, and help him look out for Camdyn.'"

"Hmm..." A giggle slid out as I glanced at him. "I honestly don't recall saying those words."

"They were there."

"Huh." I turned my focus back to Camdyn, still standing next to my father in her pale yellow dress, hair halfway up with a small section of curls cascading over her shoulders, completely oblivious to the people looking at her.

Naturally, those people included the man she brought as her date. He sat alone at another table, brooding over his empty champagne flute.

"I guess you'll need all the help you can get in that department," I finally told my husband.

"What's that poor guy's name again?"

"Jamie. You know, if I squint really hard, he kind of looks like Clark Kent."

Charlie laughed quietly next to my ear. "Clark Kent morphs into Superman, though. I'm pretty sure that guy is always...that version. Anyway, you can't help but feel sorry for the poor sap."

"He was only coming as a friend in the first place," I explained. "She wanted to un-invite him after he started acting interested in her romantically, but he already had the plane ticket."

Charlie grunted next to me as he placed an arm around my shoulders. "I just hope her chaotic life doesn't leave a mess in the wake again. Did you talk to her about coming back home?"

"I always do. She was almost done with her book research, so she said she might be moving soon. I'd say she's open to the idea, as soon as there's a catalyst to get her into motion."

"Don't say that too loud. It could be a disaster."

"Your dad thinks an awesome curveball has that distinction because the ball is spinning forward and creates unequal pressure between the top and the bottom," Camdyn informed us as she suddenly appeared across from me at the table. "Since the bottom of the baseball has the lower amount of pressure, there's a downward force caused."

"Um, he's probably right?" I suggested.

As she slowly shook her head, Charlie placed his arm around my shoulders, as though I still had a lot to learn about baseball. Granted, my love for that had never blossomed, but I wasn't about to argue over my dad knowing physics. It was his thing, after all.

"Trina, you can't be serious," Camdyn said. "There is such a thing as a clutch pitcher, you know. He's not thinking about physics, he's just crazy talented. I thought you were explaining all this to her, Charlie."

"He tries."

Rather than make fun of me, Charlie pulled me closer and kissed my temple. "Why don't you come back to St. Louis so we can go to the games together, Cam? That will save Trina from the headache of pretending she likes baseball."

"Please," I begged, making a pouty face as I twined my fingers together in front of my face.

"Don't guilt me. You know I can't stand that." She twisted her head to glance at Jamie, and then returned her gaze to me with a slight grimace on her face. "How totally awkward is this? I feel rather bad for ignoring him, but I don't want him to get the wrong idea."

Having only been introduced to Jamie the night before at the rehearsal dinner, I barely knew the guy. He seemed polite, and Camdyn had told me a couple times about their lively discussions, since he was a history professor at one of the local colleges where she lived.

"He's coming over here," Charlie stated.

Her eyes widened as Jamie tapped on her shoulder, and she slowly turned around.

"Care to dance?"

Camdyn offered him a gracious smile and rose to take his hand, appearing not to want to hurt his feelings. It made me feel slightly proud of her, and I turned to look at Charlie.

"I'm pretty sure she'll be okay," I said. "Anyway, there are more important things to think about, like picking out new appliances so I can use Willa's recipes."

"If you get new appliances, you'll have to repaint the kitchen."

"Something bright and sunny, so it would fit the vibe of the house."

He nodded his agreement as he took my hand. "You're sure you don't want a nicer house, sweetheart? With my new job, it wouldn't be any trouble finding something else. The fact that Grandma left it to me doesn't mean we have to live there."

"I can't imagine living anywhere else." I lifted his hand and placed both mine around his, rubbing my finger across the new ring he was wearing. "I found joy there, and hope, and...you. If we live the whole of our lives in that little house, you playing baseball in the backyard with the kids and me making cookies in the kitchen, I'd be perfectly content."

He leaned forward to kiss me, leaving his head against my forehead when he was finished. "I'm pretty sure everything about that little speech would make Grandma smile."

♥

"May I have your attention please?" The distinct sound of a fork clinking against a glass rang out across the banquet hall, and Charlie squeezed my hand under the table as we turned our attention to Camdyn, who was standing in front of the microphone, looking slightly embarrassed. As confident as she seemed in everyday conversation, she couldn't stand speaking in front of a crowd. In fact, beyond her wide-eyed countenance, I saw the beginnings of a blush creeping into her cheeks.

"I've been told that I'm supposed to say a few words about Trina and Charlie," she began, glancing over at us. "I wish I would have known ahead of time. I would have prepared something." Unclasping her fist, she let a roll of paper slip downward, where it continued to unroll until it draped across the floor. The crowd giggled, and she looked over at me and winked. "You all think that was a grand joke, but Trina is worried right now that I have written on every inch of this paper. And her worries are founded, because I have."

Charlie groaned, and I poked him in the side. Camdyn was my best friend and now my sister-in-law, so although his teasing about her quirky traits usually made me laugh, at that moment I was feeling somewhat sentimental.

"Trina Justine Miller stepped into my life on a cold January day, breezing into my dorm room like a breath of summer air. She tossed a canvas bag on the bed and asked me what I was reading. I promptly told her that I was contemplating strategy by Burnside at the Battle of Antietam, and her eyes glazed over. Luckily for me, I happened to have a snack size package of Oreos. Unable to think of anything to follow my history announcement, I wordlessly offered her my snack. She's been following me around ever since."

I remembered that day well. She was cross-legged on her bed and had a pencil holding her bun in place on top of her head. When she started rattling off things about strategy, I thought she was talking about one of those reality television shows. We had a good laugh about it.

"Things seemed to be going well for me at the time, but once Trina came into my life, I knew they couldn't go back to the way they were. Even though it seems like we don't have much in common, Trina and I were designed to be kindred spirits. She was destined to be family to me from the moment I met her. I had no idea how literal that thought would turn out to be.

"There was a time when the idea of Trina and Charlie made me anything but happy. It was Christmas Day, and Trina had come to stay with us because her parents were in Florida and she wanted pumpkin pie. Wow, Trina, I never realized before how much your life revolves around food."

Laughter helped ward off my embarrassment, but I couldn't help but glance toward Aunt Shelly while I thought about her seafood Christmas. My step-cousin Todd caught my eye, and I doubted that kid had ever stopped growing. He was practically predestined to be a center for the Miami Heat.

"I'll never forget it, because I was sitting on the couch in my pajamas, we were opening gifts, and suddenly there was this moment happening between the two of them. It was palpable, really, and I felt it before I knew what was going on. I looked up to see him crossing the room, giving her a hug, and I was pretty sure I'd just lost my friend to my brother. Feeling devastated, I immediately dubbed it the worst Christmas ever."

"Notice she didn't mention anything about kicking the couch and barely being able to walk after," Charlie whispered as he leaned close.

"No doubt she wants to forget that," I answered, nestling further into the crook of his arm.

"Well, I was wrong," Camdyn continued, her focus moving from her paper to me and Charlie. "That was the best Christmas ever, because it was the one and only Christmas where my entire family was present. The next year, Trina spent the holidays with her parents in Nebraska. The year after that, my grandma was gone."

She paused for a moment to collect herself, and I knew how hard that was for her to say. Willa's death had devastated her, and she still hadn't recovered. My heart hurt for her.

"So in my memories, that worst Christmas now ranks right up there with the most wonderful memories I have. All the people I loved were under one roof, sneaking around behind my back, but together all the same." She hesitated a couple seconds as she offered us a smile. "Trina has been my sister from the very beginning. Thank you, Charlie, for making it official." Grabbing a glass from the table behind her, she held it aloft. "To Charlie and Trina. May I dream of one day having a love so perfect."

"To Charlie and Trina," the crowd repeated.

She walked over to us, and Charlie rose and put his arms around her. They stood there together for a moment, him talking quietly while she nodded, no doubt giving her some brotherly encouragement. He had been worried about her since she disappeared after Willa's funeral, and although she seemed to have her head on her shoulders a bit more as the years passed, he still wanted to protect her.

I loved that about him.

"Trina," she said as she shifted to stand before me, adjusting the top of her dress. "You've been the best... I love you."

"I love you, too." Wrapping my arms around her neck, I held on tight. "Thanks for sharing life with me. I couldn't enjoy it more if I had a million dollars and a rope of diamonds."

"You're quoting *Anne of Green Gables* to me?"

"I've heard it enough," I stated with a laugh as she took a step back. Smiling, she handed me the roll of paper, and I glanced down at it and started unrolling. Once I had about two feet open, I glanced up at her and shook my head.

"What?" she asked, looking rather sly. "It worked."

Staring back at the paper, I couldn't help but laugh. In the center, written in large red letters, was one simple word: RELAX.

"I guess that means it's my turn," Charlie's friend Eli stated, assuming the microphone as best man. Camdyn and I halted our conversation to look in his direction just in time for both our expressions to change: mine to one of surprise, and hers to what appeared to be dread.

"Actually, if I could just take a minute," Camdyn's date Jamie interrupted, removing the microphone from Eli's hand. "Hey. Hello. Beautiful wedding. Beautiful." His words were noticeably slurred and he seemed rather unsteady, as though he were visibly drunk.

"We only gave out one glass of champagne for toasting," I whispered.

"What? He's not supposed to drink with his medication."

"Did someone tell *him*?"

"I need to say a few words about that lady," Jamie rattled on, pointing in our general direction, his finger roaming about like he couldn't focus it in one spot. "She's fan-tastic. Perfect even. Mag-nifi..." Pausing, he began fumbling in his pocket. "...cent. She deserves true love. *Love.* Yes, she does."

"My life is over," Camdyn mumbled.

With one deft move, he jerked a black ring box out of his pocket and flicked it open with one finger, comically like something on a slapstick movie. The desire to laugh rose within me, but I didn't dare with Camdyn standing so close.

"Camdyn, you are really hot. Really hot. And you just... You get me. You *under-stand* me."

Apparently having had enough, Camdyn rushed in his direction, nearly tumbling over the edge of the table in the process. As she began removing the microphone from his hand and handing it back to Eli, her words could be clearly heard throughout the room.

"Okay, Jamie, let's get you some fresh air. Obviously, you're confused. Would you just be quiet? I'm trying to help you preserve your dignity. For goodness sake, put that ring back in your pocket."

"Man, I really should have put that thing in the vows about watching Camdyn," Charlie said beside me as he pulled me against him. "It's definitely going to take the two of us."

"It might take a village," I corrected, smiling up at my husband. "But we'll start with two and take it from there."

"You're really good for her, you know that?" Leaning down, he gave me a quick kiss.

"And good for you, too. That's what Willa told me that Christmas Eve."

"Really? She told me the same thing the night we did the drop and dash." He offered a charming smile as he nodded and looked up. "Thanks, Grandma. You were right, just like always."

"And when did *you* start thinking I was good for you?" I asked, feeling completely at home in his arms.

"When I opened your gift that Christmas. It felt like I had just unwrapped the future."

ACKNOWLEDGEMENTS

Thank you to Mike for answering my random, odd questions. To Reinah, for helping me name characters with her active imagination. To Truett, for giving me a glimpse of what it might have been like to have a brother. To my family and friends who are my first line of defense and help to make the stories better. I'm grateful for each of you.

Special thanks to Erica, my cover photographer, and to Brittany, for agreeing to portray Trina. You both made my job easy.

When I started daydreaming about Camdyn Taylor, I never would have imagined all the stories I'd get to tell through her family. All thanks goes to God, because He created these terrific characters and plopped them into my mind, fully formed. They have become like family to me, so coming back to them felt like coming home.

ABOUT THE AUTHOR

Christina Coryell is the Amazon bestselling author of The Camdyn Series and the Girls of Wonder Lane series. She holds degrees in English and History from Drury University and resides in southwest Missouri with her husband and two children. She does most of her writing in unorthodox places and with lots of noise in the background.

She knows what it means to have kindred spirit friends—her best friend on the first day of kindergarten was her best friend on the last day of high school. You can find her at www.christinacoryell.com.